Samantha sat up and moved so she could reach his left leg and, without speaking, began massaging. Her strong fingers pressed into the muscles. Nicholas made no sound as she worked her way to his ankle, feeling for tenderness. Taking his right foot in her hand, she rubbed upward to his thigh, tensed beneath her hands.

He caught her shoulders, pulling her up to him, his hands moving quickly to help remove her clothing. She tried to roll away from him, but he held her.

"I'm afraid I'll hurt you," she whispered.

"No, you won't hurt me; you'll love me...."

ABOUT THE AUTHOR

Zelma Orr had a most interesting career before turning to writing full-time: she was a U.S. Customs Officer for the Treasury Department in her home state of Texas. Zelma loves to travel and keeps a diary of the places she's been to use for story ideas for future books.

Books by Zelma Orr

Measure
of Love

ZELMA ORR

Harlequin Books

TORONTO • NEW YORK • LONDON
AMSTERDAM • PARIS • SYDNEY • HAMBURG
STOCKHOLM • ATHENS • TOKYO • MILAN

Published December 1984

ISBN 0-373-16082-8

Printed in Canada

Chapter One

The hours between two and six in the morning were generally quiet in the orthopedic ward, and Samantha gratefully used the time to stay at her desk doing catch-up work. The flow of paper was never-ending as she recorded the dispensing of painkillers, shots, and pills. If she could keep that ornery little Benjamin Carter in his bed, she'd be ninety-nine percent finished with her night's work. No matter how many times she put the pillows around him to keep him from rolling, he could still pull his thin legs from the padded wire supports. She had never been able to figure out how he could get out of the restraints without breaking every bone in his small body. He was a very determined five-year-old.

With a sigh Samantha closed her books and stood up to stretch. Her graveyard shift would end at seven in the morning, giving her four days off before she began her next tour. She would be free to do as she pleased and she meant to put it to good use for Christmas shopping, perhaps even for an overnight trip up Rimrock Canyon to see the changing colors. Autumn in the Cascade Mountains spread more shades of orange, red, and yellow than any color chart ever boasted. She could take pictures to send home with her Christmas presents to San Antonio where most of the trees were transplanted palms or bunchy live oaks that turned pale colors and then brown almost immediately. Not that her mother and Emily would appreciate it.

"I don't see why you have to accept a position way out there with no family around you, when there are plenty of well-paying jobs here for nurses," her mother had complained when she was accepted at Young Memorial in Yakima, Washington.

The answer to that was in her mother's complaint. Samantha would have no family around her and, as cold as that sounded, she looked forward to it. She would be away from her mother's rehashing all the reasons her older daughter should think about marrying before she was thirty, not too far in the future. Away from her sister Emily, who stood five-foot-seven, was one hundred twenty pounds of willowy sensuousness, and delighted in making reference to her amazonian sister.

The worst part was Emily was so right. Her mother's half-hearted protests that Samantha was big-boned, big-framed, and naturally built big did nothing to change her five-foot-ten, one-hundred-seventy-pound dimensions. A sunny, frequent smile that brought dancing lights to her hazel eyes on a regular basis and sandy-blond hair were plusses for her that Emily ignored when she looked her over with her taunting smile.

"Where will she ever find a man big enough for her, Mums?" She moved with catlike grace across the room, her jeans hugging each move with threads clinging lovingly to her hips.

With Herculean effort Samantha would refrain from planting her size eights firmly in her sister's shapely rear. The conversations were always the same, and for that reason her trips home to San Antonio were few and far between.

The call light came on a door down the hall, and she turned quickly to answer it, almost stumbling over the small figure outside the door.

"Benjamin!" she exclaimed as she righted herself and stooped beside him.

Bright eyes twinkled at her as he lifted his arms. "Carry me," he said.

"You know I can't, Benjy. Stay right there till I get help." Muttering to herself, Samantha turned back to the button that would summon her a stretcher.

To lift him in her arms would be easy. But in doing so she could stretch the soft bones and undo the progress they had made in treating the disease that drained the calcium from his bones more quickly than they could restore it.

"Oh, Harve," she said. "Thank goodness you answered so quickly. Help me get Benjy back to his room."

The orderly, summoned many times for this same task, bent with her and together they supported the small body, sliding Benjy gently onto the stretcher, and rolling him down the hall.

As they transferred him back into his bed, they saw Benjy put out his hand and his lips tremble. Trying not to let her sympathy show, Samantha pulled the wire mesh frames around him and, as she did so, took his hand and held it to her, smiling into his eyes. Leaning closer to straighten his pillow, she brushed her lips across his cheek and was rewarded with a tremulous smile.

"You'll be the death of me yet, Benjamin Carter," she scolded, her voice tender. "Promise me you'll stay in bed."

"Can I have some hot chocolate if I do?" he asked.

She laughed. "You're nothing but a con man, but just for you," she promised.

Samantha brought the hot chocolate and continued her rounds, leaving the floor in good shape for her morning relief. Changing into street clothes, she removed her handbag from the locker and walked down the empty back hallway, taking the shortcut past the conference room at the end of the building to get to the nurses' dormitory.

"Oh, Miss Bridges, do you have a moment?" Myers Reston, the director of administration, stood in the doorway to the conference room.

What did I do now? Samantha wondered. Myers Reston was not one to stop a registered nurse obviously on her way home from a long night shift.

"Yes, Dr. Reston?"

He cleared his throat and smiled. "If you're not in too big a hurry, we have a problem we'd like to discuss with you."

Like stop babying Benjamin Carter, she thought, as she stepped through the doorway to face Ida Vincent, the superintendent of nurses for Young Memorial. Two of the big shots together at this time of morning spelled trouble for someone—Samantha Bridges, in particular. She could feel it in her bones just like the change of weather.

Dr. Reston picked up a pencil from the conference table and turned it in his fingers before glancing at Mrs. Vincent, then at Samantha.

"We have a request from one of the big lumber companies in the timbered area above Bumping River, where there was a fire last week. They have a badly injured employee who can't be moved and need a nurse to stay and care for him until they can get him to a hospital." He paused and studied Samantha's face. "They asked for a male nurse, but there's none available from here. Since the call is urgent, we feel we shouldn't keep shunting them around to other places where they might locate a male nurse." He stopped, waiting for her reaction.

And I'm the next best thing, she thought grimly, getting the gist of what he was saying. She asked the obvious anyway. "And where do I fit in, Dr. Reston?"

He cleared his throat again. "Since you're the best nurse in the area, we were hoping you might agree to go and stay with the man until someone else can be located. We'll keep looking, of course."

The best, not to mention the biggest. *And of course,* she thought sweetly, *you'll keep looking like my Aunt Hootnannie.*

"I'm just coming off the eleven-to-seven shift, and I'm due four days off, Dr. Reston. I feel that I need that time off to catch up on rest before I go to another job.''

He nodded. ''I understand, Miss Bridges. Unfortunately the need is for right now, as soon as arrangements can be made for you to leave.''

''I assume arrangements have already been made?'' She was tired, and being shoved into an assignment without even a by-your-leave wasn't sitting too well with her. She needed a vacation, not isolated duty.

Ida Vincent spoke. ''Forgive me, Samantha, but I recommended you to Dr. Reston. We know we can depend on you, and from what small amount of information we got from the representative of the company requesting the nurse, it is a tough assignment since you'll be alone and it's a man you'll be caring for. That was their reason for the original request for a male nurse, but they say they'll take what they can get because it's very important.''

She leaned toward Samantha who winced at her comment. ''The man was hurt fighting the fire near Goose Prairie, and the report said he was badly injured, bones broken in several places. A company doctor is in attendance at the cabin, but there are others to care for and he can't remain with this man constantly.'' She smiled. ''The salary they quoted was outstanding.''

Samantha eyed her warily. Ida Vincent was good to her, always giving her the highest of evaluations. But then, she always got the best service from Samantha, too, because she always did her best. Still if the salary was as high as Ida indicated, she could pay off the new van she was so proud of and had planned to try out in Rimrock Canyon on her days off.

"Do you have any idea how long the assignment will last?" she asked.

Dr. Reston shook his head. "As soon as the man can be moved, he'll be flown to the nearest hospital with a bone specialist team, I'm sure."

"How far is he from Yakima?" she asked.

"Northwest of Cliffdell, toward Goose Prairie."

She drew in a deep breath. "They'd better get him out of there soon, or he'll be snowed in for the winter. I, for one, would not like to be stuck way up there."

Dr. Reston laughed. "There are a few more weeks of good weather." He leaned forward. "What about it, Miss Bridges? Can we call them back and tell them you'll go?"

She nodded and rose to go. "Don't forget you owe me four days off when I get back."

He came around the desk to shake her hand. "Of course. I want you to know we appreciate your doing this on such short notice."

Samantha wasn't sure she still had her right mind to agree to the assignment. "Is it a place I can drive into or do I have to walk?"

He smiled again. "I hear you have a new four-wheel-drive van that should be just the vehicle to take you into the area. A messenger is due to drop off a map to the place tonight, and I'll give it to you in the morning as you're ready to leave."

She had been on odd private-duty assignments before, so this one wouldn't be much different except for the fact that she was filling in for an unavailable male nurse.

"I sincerely wish you'd been able to find one, Mr.

Whoever-you-are,'' she mumbled to herself as she
packed heavier than usual clothing. October up on
Bumping River could be chilly. At least she'd get to see
a change of autumn colors but doubted there were
shopping malls to do her Christmas shopping.

She looked around her dormitory room at the comfortable area she spent little time in. Either she was
working or off rambling in the mountains, where she
loved to stay overnight or all weekend when she could.
The recent purchase of the van gave her a lot of oppor-
tunities to stay at campgrounds with hookups, something she had learned to use with Leo's help.

Samantha smiled thinking of Leo Jarvis, one of the
newer doctors to arrive at Young. Their time off together could be called dating, she supposed, certain
that the staff referred to them as the odd couple. Leo,
almost as tall as she and about half as wide, at least had
a wonderful sense of humor, and they enjoyed the
open spaces away from the problems of the hospital.

Opening drawers and her closet, she checked to see
what she could take that would be appropriate for a
week in the wilderness near Goose Prairie with unpre-
dictable fall weather. All she remembered about the
area was a narrow dirt road that went off into nowhere.
What in the world was a logger doing on Bumping
River? There weren't enough big trees to interest a big
company she was sure. Why would he be fighting
forest fires when they had experienced fire fighters for
that job?

Samantha pulled out brown knit pants and a beige
bulky knit sweater, two slipover shirts, and a red down
jacket—and checked to see that the red woolen tobog-

gan cap was still in the pocket—then added black pants
and boots. Just for good measure, she included a uniform, oxfords, and a heavy sweater to wear over the
outfit. The jeans she bought the past summer were too
tight across her rear end, so she reached instead for the
navy wool pants and navy pullover. They didn't make
her look any smaller, but the dark colors didn't em-
phasize the heaviness through her breasts and shoulders.

She sighed. Someday, she promised herself, she
would go to one of those medical weight-loss clinics
that guaranteed a loss of forty pounds or your money
back. All the diets and exercise programs she went on
herself did nothing but irritate her and the hospital dietitian. The last one they worked out lasted six months,
and she gained four pounds, much to her disgust. The
dietitian accused her of cheating and Samantha lost her
temper, remembering how she starved and listened to
her stomach growling in protest when she refused to fill
it up except with carrots and celery.

"I'll never eat another carrot or celery stick as long
as I live," she told the dismayed dietitian as she
stormed out of the hospital kitchen and, true to her
word, she hadn't since that time.

What she had done was to go into town one day and
sit for a consultation with a new outfit that guaranteed
no starving and no strenuous exercise. She walked
through the ultra-modern slenderizing salon with the
bony hostess, watching in amazement as women lay on
what looked like skeletal hospital beds covered in black
leatherlike material, their legs propped at awkward
angles as the machines bumped and rolled them while

they lay relaxed. The hostess discussed the way she wanted her to eat and the times allowed on the machines each day and quoted her a price. Samantha silently whistled at the amount but agreed to try the machine.

She was left alone after the slender woman showed her how to position herself on the machine and turned the switch for a half hour's motion. Samantha held on to the sides of the narrow bed as the machine went to work.

With her thighs angled where she could see them, she watched the excess flesh as it shook and wiggled with the motion of the machine. Simple amazement kept her quiet for the twenty-minute cycle, but when the machine shifted into a faster pace and her entire body oscillated with alarming speed until she thought she would be catapulted into space, she began to giggle silently and couldn't stop. When the fashionably slim hostess returned to see how she was doing, the tears were running down her cheeks and the girl gazed at her doubtfully.

"Are you hurt? The machines are guaranteed not to injure," she assured her, helping Samantha from the table.

Shaking her head and unable to speak, Samantha made her way outside to her car where she collapsed over the steering wheel until she could control her laughter. Shaking her head, she started her car, muttering to herself and occasionally going into fits of laughter.

Eating a sandwich later in the cafeteria with Leo, she related the story to him and both of them went into gales of laughter. Leo was thin enough not to have to worry about overeating, and Samantha gained if she inhaled ether.

"I might as well forget trying to lose weight," she told him. "I've always been fat, and I guess I always will be."

"You're not fat, Samantha," he said, looking her over. "A little bigger than some around here, but not fat."

"Come on, Leo," she admonished him. "But, thanks, anyway."

She really should be used to being heavy, having been compared to Emily all her life, but she guessed she'd probably always wish she weren't quite so richly endowed.

"You've got a great sense of humor. Besides, you'd be surprised at how grouchy some of the skinny girls can get," Leo said.

"Fat people aren't always happy," she told him, "regardless of what you're told."

"Are you unhappy?" Leo asked.

She thought about it a second and answered truthfully. "No, thank goodness. I'm quite happy, as a matter of fact."

"Well, then?"

She grinned across at him. "So I stay, shall we say, just a little heftier than I'd like to be."

Samantha smiled now, thinking of Leo. He always understood her—even if she was a heavyweight.

With her packing completed she showered and lay across her bed, waiting to hear from Dr. Reston. Maybe they'd find a male nurse in the meantime and wouldn't need her, she thought drowsily, but the next thing she knew a knock woke her. She struggled to her feet and sat still for a moment before walking half-asleep to the door. "Who is it?"

"Ida Vincent."

Samantha opened the door, pushing her hair from her face. "Come in, Mrs. Vincent," she invited and stepped aside as the woman entered.

"The messenger left this map, Samantha, and said the doctor would be in the cabin until you get there. Do you know this area?"

She took the map and studied it. "Yes, I was near Cliffdell a couple of weeks ago. I've never been farther than American River, and that's barely a wide place in the road. What was a logger doing up there?"

"He wasn't one of their regular loggers and just happened to be there when the fire broke out and helped fight when it got out of control. Dr. Knight, the company doctor, is there with him and can tell you how he needs to be handled."

Samantha nodded as she followed the red line on the map that told her which route to take. She guessed it was about fifty miles from Yakima. The roads were good at least until the turnoff just before American River. She couldn't vouch for what the narrow lane would be like from there to the cabin, but she wasn't afraid to venture onto it with the new four-wheel-drive van.

The brief nap, short as it was, had helped and she felt refreshed as she locked her room behind her and carried the suitcase down to the van, stopping by the lobby to drop a note in Leo's mail slot to let him know she'd be gone for a few days.

When she was finally settled behind the wheel, she felt a shiver of apprehension. Samantha knew the area well enough, that was true, but her mind was nevertheless filled with wonder about the patient who awaited her.

Chapter Two

Heading northwest out of town, Samantha breathed in the fresh crispness of the October morning and her spirits lifted. She might have to work for a grumpy old fire fighter, but she could enjoy the scenery while she was at it. Nothing suited her more than to get away from the city and into the uninterrupted quiet of the mountains, the only noise that of the trickling streams or smooth-flowing unpolluted rivers.

From Cliffdell the terrain elevated sharply and rugged mountains towered over her. Half an hour later, she made a sharp turn and saw the small sign: "American River—3 miles." She stopped to look once more at the map.

The bridge she had just crossed was over the Naches River and to her left was a smaller stream she knew was Bumping River. The red arrow on the map indicated a left turn just before the general store in American River, population probably totaling two families— maybe. She couldn't recall ever seeing anyone nearby.

Around her the trees whispered in the light breeze, and she watched a squirrel streak along to the trunk of a

large redwood where he sat on his hind legs a moment
before disappearing into the low underbrush. The
touches of gold and scarlet through the heavy foliage
heralded the change in the seasons that Samantha
loved. San Antonio went from hot and humid to cool
and humid, seldom very cold. She loved the changes
and never tired of the scenery from the relative flatness
of Yakima to over six thousand feet where she now sat.

With one last glance at it, she folded the piece of
paper and slipped it into her jacket pocket, pulling the
van back onto the narrow road. Around a curve she
came upon a weathered post with a faded sign that read:
"Goose Prairie—12 miles" and stopped again, looking
ahead down the road toward American River, wondering if she should see what was there now or go on up
toward the cabin she was supposed to find. Deciding
against American River, she turned onto the gravel
trail, heading in the direction the sign pointed to Goose
Prairie. The map said the cabin was just off the trail
about five miles away.

Thank goodness she didn't have to drive twelve
miles on this excuse for a road, she thought as she
started up again.

Hairpin turns and straight-up elevations claimed
her undivided attention as she maneuvered the easy-
handling van, thankful again that she had finally decided she could handle the debt of the balance between
her old car and the new van she had put off buying for
so long. It was definitely a joy to drive in this rough
territory.

Another sharp turn brought her into sight of a log
cabin nestled in the tall pines. A truck was parked in

the small clearing that served as a yard. Guiding the van into the space near the truck, Samantha switched off the motor and gazed around, her eyes appreciating the beauty of the isolated wilderness.

The door to the cabin opened and a man came toward her, walking quickly. She climbed out of the van and went to meet him.

"I'm Dr. Knight," the man said, his hand outstretched.

"Samantha Bridges, Doctor," she told him. "From Young Memorial," she added, in case he had any doubts someone other than such a refugee could find herself in this wilderness for some other purpose.

Behind thick glasses his eyes went over her and he cleared his throat.

Uh-oh, she thought. He sounded like Dr. Reston and that always meant trouble. He nodded as if in agreement with the unspoken statement. "Dr. Reston told me he wasn't able to find a male nurse but you were the best he had, which is what we need here."

"That bad?" she asked, not wanting to hear his answer.

"Yes." He turned and she fell into step with him. He was taller than she was, at least, if not broader. "Mr. Jordan has multiple fractures of his left leg, a dislocated shoulder, and contusions of the right arm and leg." He glanced at her. "Also a slight concussion."

She stopped. "I hate to ask this, but if he was brought this far, why wasn't he transported at least to Naches where medical people could reach him?"

He stopped, too, reluctantly she thought, before he answered. "We were unable to reach him for a while after the accident, and this is as far as we dared take him." He looked around and pointed. "That's where the fire came to, and there were only four of them to fight it. He was driving a tractor, providing a break, when he hit a tree trunk hidden under the brush and the tractor turned over partly on him."

Samantha flinched. She was familiar with farm and vehicle injuries and they were never pretty. "I see." She turned to look toward the small log cabin, smoke curling from a big rock chimney at one end.

"Mr. Jordan is unconscious. Well, actually he's semiconscious."

She swung around. "Unconscious? And you plan to leave us isolated here with little medical advice? And what about emergency conditions? As if this isn't emergency enough."

He held up his hand and for the first time, she noticed the fatigue around his mouth, the slump to his shoulders. "I'm sorry, Miss Bridges, but I'm the only doctor that's available, and I have more injured to take care of in these hills if I can find them. The fire gutted the area and has just been brought under control. Even if we had the means to move Mr. Jordan, he can't be moved without doing permanent damage to his leg. I've been told it will not be done."

Dr. Knight took off his glasses and rubbed his eyes. "You come well recommended." He smiled a little. "Believe me, you were given a good screening before being allowed to come here, so I have confidence in you. It's a job, I know, but we're depending on you."

"What do you mean 'screened'?"

"Mr. Jordan's company places a lot of value on

him," he said dryly, turning to the door and opening it to let her walk into the dim interior of the cabin.

Samantha's eyes narrowed at the doctor's statements. She had been screened before; that didn't bother her. But who was this company that thought it could pry into someone's private life in order to obtain her services? There was such a thing as invasion of privacy, in case they hadn't yet heard.

Turning her thoughts more to her present problem, she gazed around her with not a little trepidation. It was a neat room, sparsely furnished. In the corner was a wood range and nearby was a refrigerator. From the heavy wooden ceiling beams a light bulb dangled from a cord.

"Where do they get electricity this far out?"

"There's a powerful generator, but the people who use the cabin didn't want to risk an electric stove, so they have the wood range. There's plenty of wood out back." He smiled apologetically. "I don't imagine you've had much experience with wood stoves."

Samantha surveyed the room, inventorying the simple items, not about to tell him she could build a camp fire with the best of the outdoorsmen. Let him think she was helpless in some ways; maybe he wouldn't leave her here very long without someone to check on her.

"I can probably manage," she said. "What are you feeding Mr. Jordan if he's unconscious?"

"Intravenously until today; he finally took a little soup. Supplies are in the pantry on the back porch, and I'm sure you'll be out of here before they're all used up. Just make sure you keep plenty of liquids in him."

Dr. Knight went to a small table in the corner and picked up two medical bags. "I'll leave this bag for you. It has the equipment for giving the shots for pain and capsules when he can swallow more easily. There'll be someone to see about you in a couple of days, Miss Bridges."

He turned toward the closed door leading into the other room, motioning her to follow him. A fire built into a big rock fireplace at the end of the room was the source of the smoke she had seen from outside. A built-in bunk was against the entire length of the opposite wall. Over the top of the bunk, an apparatus for holding broken bones had been installed by some enterprising person, presumably Dr. Knight. Wider than a normal cabin bunk, the built-in was completely covered by the figure occupying it.

Samantha walked closer and looked down at the injured Mr. Jordan. *Heavens to Betsy,* she thought, her eyes widening. *I always pictured Paul Bunyan as having black hair.*

The man she stared at was blond, his hair shaggy, a heavy beard mixed dark and light streaks. Firmly molded lips were slightly parted and dry, showing fever. Thick dark lashes lay against the small amount of tanned cheek that showed signs of being too close to the flames. His nose was peeling.

Her glance went over his body. His shoulder was wrapped in a homemade sling, holding his left arm close to his chest. Dark blond hairs covered the back of the huge fist clenched as though he were in pain. A sheet covered the portion of his body not hooked to the containing harness, and she realized he was naked except for the bandages. She swallowed. This was not the old fire fighter she'd thought he would be but a man about as big as she had ever seen. He was over six feet tall and two hundred forty pounds.

"Where's his purple ox?" she muttered to herself.

"I'm sorry, what did you say?" Dr. Knight asked behind her.

Samantha turned, slightly dazed at the appearance of her patient. "Do I need to turn him or adjust the harness at any given time?"

"Yes," he said, "like this." He proceeded to tell her and show the workings of the apparatus, as Samantha nodded, familiar enough with the delicate handling of broken and healing bones to understand what he was saying.

"What if he develops a very high fever?" she asked, already believing she was out of her mind to agree to this assignment and wondering how she could get out of it gracefully. She knew the answer to that. If Ida Vincent and Dr. Myers Reston asked her to take on a job, it was a job to see through until the end—regardless.

"There's alcohol for rubs and these lotions to prevent sores. Use them until we can get him where they have the equipment to turn him without injury."

She nodded, looking down at the giant-sized figure of the man in the bunk. "How long do you think that will be?"

"A week, ten days at the most." He turned to go back through the next room and Samantha followed him to the door. "I'll be back in a few days to check on him—and you," he added as an afterthought. He held out his hand and said, "I appreciate your agreeing to come up and look out for Mr. Jordan, and I know his employer will, too." His moves were weary as he got into the truck, waved, and pulled away down the narrow trail.

With loads of misgiving, Samantha stood watching the tailgate of the truck and saw the lights come on as it began to back up. As he came close to her, Dr. Knight leaned out the window.

"I forgot, Miss Bridges," he said. "Mr. Jordan's dog Hannibal is wandering around the woods somewhere. She'll be in by dinnertime; she's always hungry. There's dog food in the pantry." He pulled away before she could summon an answer to the newest problem.

"Damn!" she fumed aloud for no one to hear. "Paul Bunyan doesn't have a purple ox, so he saddles me with a dog. There were plenty of male nurses available; they just had more sense than to come up here for this...this..." Words failed her as she tried to describe the situation, then turned to the van to remove her suitcase, taking the sleeping bag she kept in the van as an afterthought.

The late afternoon air was becoming cooler, so Samantha removed stove-sized wood from the box in the corner and arranged it in the stove, using the small pieces as kindling. There were long wooden matches in a jar on the table and it took only two before she had the fire going.

Opening the refrigerator, she checked the contents: margarine, a jar of powdered milk, several cartons of eggs, cheese, two loaves of wheat bread, mustard, and ketchup. Still investigating, she saw that the door to the back was locked with a double chain, so she slid it back to open it and walked out onto the porch. To her left was a pantry, its shelves loaded with a generous supply of assorted canned goods, one shelf almost completely dog food including a bag of some sort of burger bits. Samantha opened another door to discover a miniature bathroom, complete with a tiny shower stall.

"Hooray," she said, "modern conveniences."

Shaking her head at what she might find next, she turned to face the ugliest dog she ever hoped to see. They stared at each other, Samantha with her mouth wide open.

"Hannibal, I presume."

The animal weighed at least fifty pounds and had enough wrinkled skin on her forehead and under her eyes to furnish two more dogs. Her thick muzzle was a dark brown that looked like a man's five-o'clock shadow against the honey-blond coat on the rest of her. All Samantha remembered about dogs was their round dark eyes, but the eyes on this one were gold-colored, triangle-shaped, sharply pointed at the top, or maybe all the skin folded there caused them to look that way.

Hannibal looked her over much the same way, and she decided that she must be as odd-looking to the dog as the dog was to her. The animal moved closer to her, sniffing her pants leg. After a moment the dog sat, putting forth one of the thick paws for her to shake.

"Mannerly, anyway," Samantha said, extending her hand to the dog and withdrawing it self-consciously when she realized what she had done. She wiped her hand on her pants and backed away as the dog watched, evidently insulted that she would wipe her hand after a handshake with such a thoroughbred lady.

"I guess you live inside, too?" she asked as the dog followed closely at her heels.

The dog wandered over to the closed door of the room where her master lay and flopped with a long sigh, her sadly wrinkled face spread on her legs. The wrinkles heretofore had been confined to the face but as the dog lay down, her legs and body became a mass of loose skin that was somehow attached to the muscular frame. She closely resembled a pile of golden rags.

"I'm asking for double pay to care for both of you," she told the unconcerned animal. "Whatever happens from here on in is bound to be more than I bargained for." With that prophecy spoken aloud for the record, she looked around the room once more and went toward the door where Hannibal lay.

The knob turned quietly beneath her long fingers, and Samantha moved to the side of the wide bunk where Nicholas Jordan lay. She took the chart from the table and sat down in the straight chair by the bed. She groaned at the complicated broken bones listed there and looked more than once at the face of the man she was to care for. She reached to touch his forehead and was pleased to find it only slightly warm. Her fingers moved over the unshaven cheek, dry and bristly. Of their own accord, her fingers touched his lips, and she quickly withdrew them as the warm breath brought a sudden flutter to her heartbeat.

Startled, she looked back at the closed eyes. He hadn't moved, but Samantha felt as though he had touched her body in some forbidden place. Her gaze went from the peaceful expression on his face to the bare shoulders only partly covered by the tightly wrapped cloth. His free arm was under the sheet, so she raised it to look, only to discover a towel was all he wore across his nakedness. She blushed and let the sheet drop, wondering why she felt embarrassed when she looked at naked bodies all the time. The sheet covered the half of him that wasn't jacked up to the harness that held his huge body immobile to enable the bones to knit correctly.

A glass of water was on the table, and she took it to dampen the washcloth lying there in order to wet his lips. As the moisture seeped between his lips, he moaned and murmured something.

"Mr. Jordan?" she said softly.

Heavy lashes moved slightly and her patient turned his head toward her, mumbling. The big arm beneath the sheet flexed and he groaned, frowning. Samantha pressed the wet cloth against his mouth and he lay still again. She sat there for several minutes, wetting first the cloth and then his mouth, her fingers massaging the arm he kept moving. He relaxed and she stood up to move away only to find Hannibal close at her heels, looking at the man on the bunk.

Glancing from the dog to the man, she smiled sympathetically and said, "He isn't going anywhere. You can relax."

Looking as alert as the wrinkles would allow, the dog gazed from her master to Samantha, seemed to make up her mind she could be trusted, and turned to leave the room with her.

The fire in the stove was going well and Samantha opened two cans of soup—one clear for her patient and tomato with rice for herself, found two small pots to heat it in, and put them on the back of the stove to serve later.

"You're special," she told Hannibal. "You get a big can of beef all to yourself." She emptied the contents of a can into the dog dish by the wall and watched as Hannibal sniffed it a couple of times, then gulped it down with one swift guzzle.

"You're not a dog, you're a vacuum cleaner," she told her disbelievingly.

Samantha sat at the small table and looked around, taking in the room, and a sudden thought occurred. "Where do I sleep?"

There was a big club chair left over from someone's garage sale, plus three spindly legged chairs at the small kitchen table where she sat. For the first time she noticed a small bunk bed behind the front door, certainly too small for her big frame, but she could use her sleeping bag easily enough. There were blankets stacked at the foot of the bunk, enough for several people.

"This cabin wasn't built for people the size of me and Mr. Jordan," she said aloud and looked at the dog. "Nor you."

The dog stood watching her to see what she would do next. "You know, maybe it's a good thing they left you here with me, else I'd be talking to myself out here in this wilderness." Skin drooped over the pointed eyes and Hannibal dropped where she was standing, sighing loudly. She wasted no energy, making the most of her few moves by relaxing completely, skin and all.

Samantha went to check on her patient and found he hadn't moved. She put a log on the low fire and, leaving the door partly open, went to open her luggage to unpack her clothes and hang them on the various nails she saw around the walls. There were no closets.

"I have some hangers in the van, Hannibal. Let's go get them." The dog raised herself reluctantly to follow Samantha, waiting until she backed out of the van with the hangers to turn and move with measured step back into the cabin with her.

"You and I should be on a diet, Hannibal. And it wouldn't hurt that master of yours, although I can't really tell if he's fat or just plain big."

Samantha bit her lip as the unfamiliar warmth stung her cheeks thinking about the naked man fate had placed in her care. She hung her clothing on assorted portions of the wall behind the door near the bunk and turned to put more wood in the stove.

Chapter Three

Going from the busy halls of Young Memorial to the
peaceful quiet of Bumping River was a big change, and
Samantha relaxed as she looked around the cabin. She
had been able to force half a cup of soup into Nicholas
Jordan and was eating her own bowl of nourishment
after having given Hannibal a double handful of burger
bits from the big bag in the pantry. Having instantly
disposed of the food, Hannibal now lay snoring near
the warm stove. Her patient was quiet but Samantha
ran a list of things through her mind that could happen
before she was checked on in however many days Dr.
Knight termed a "few." She had never been a pessi-
mist, but even so she could foresee how things could
possibly get a little rough for them.

Rinsing her soup bowl in the thin trickle of water
from the faucet, Samantha turned it down on the
wooden counter and put a pot of water on the stove to
heat for sterilizing and other sickroom duties.

A sound from the adjoining room sent her hurrying toward it, gasping as she entered to find Nicholas
half sitting up, his uninjured leg hanging to the floor.

Wide blue eyes stared at her from the bearded face. "Who the hell are you?" he demanded hoarsely.

"Samantha Bridges, a nurse, Mr. Jordan." She bent to lift his leg, but he stiffened and she couldn't budge it. "Mr. Jordan," she started to say when his free arm came out, pulling her to him.

"Sam," he muttered. "Sam, don't..." He groaned as his grasp toppled her over on him.

Struggling to get from beneath the heavy arm, she dropped to her knees and slid away from him. Putting her shoulder against his hip, she braced herself to lift his leg back onto the bed, fighting his arm still reaching for her. She wrapped the sheet around his leg and held onto the arm with both her hands, managing to do so only because he suddenly stopped fighting and lay still.

Breathing hard, Samantha stood looking down at the giant-sized figure. "They should supply forklifts and armor suits with cases such as you," she mumbled through clenched teeth. She was sweating as if it were July. "I'll fix you," she told the silent man.

Drawers beneath the bunk beds held linens, and she removed a heavy corded spread and carried it into the other room. The medical bag left by Dr. Knight was still sitting by the table, and she opened it to find a pair of surgical scissors. Sitting on the floor, she cut four narrow strips from the spread and folded the remaining piece to put back into the drawer. Hannibal pushed one eye open beneath her wrinkles, found nothing interesting in what Samantha was doing, and closed them again.

Samantha stood looking at the apparatus in front of

her, studying it to see what options she had in rearranging it for safety's sake—hers.

The man lay quiet as she looped the cloth around his uninjured hand and shoulder, beneath the slat at his side, and tied it. She used the same procedure to secure his good leg, making sure the sheet covered him completely as she worked. She frowned at such precautions.

What in the world is wrong with you, Samantha Bridges? she scolded herself. *You act like a candy-striper.* It was hard not to smile at some of the naive young teenagers who came to the hospital to help out and who eventually hoped to become registered nurses. It was even harder to remember that she had once been one of them. So why the bashfulness around this man? she asked herself again and, with no answer to that, shrugged as she picked up the lotion to massage the still figure.

Her hands were strong and she worked the creamy substance into the exposed portions of his skin, carefully covering all of it, even the peeling nose. She checked the harnesses and loosened them for a few minutes, retightening them as she finished rubbing the lotion over him.

Going back to the stove, she filled a cup with clear soup and went to feed him a few more spoonfuls. He turned his head away from her as she put the spoon near his lips.

"Come on, Mr. Jordan," she said. "You need plenty of nourishment."

The bunk shook as he twisted, trying to dislodge his arm and leg from his restraints, and suddenly he turned his head and she was looking into the fierce deepness of his blue eyes again.

She smiled. "Good evening."

"Who the hell are you?" he demanded.

"You've already asked that question. I'm Samantha Bridges, a nurse sent to care for you until you can be moved to a hospital."

His eyes went over her, touching every inch of her hair and face, down to the long, slender fingers wrapped around the cup she was holding. Her face colored under his silent scrutiny, and she wet her lips. His gaze followed the move and lingered on her mouth.

He frowned. "Sam?"

"Samantha," she corrected him.

The blue eyes held hers and he grinned. "Sam," he repeated and went to sleep.

She waited a moment, then placed the spoon near his mouth again, but he turned away and she didn't try to force him to take any more. A few spoonfuls at regular intervals would be better than forcing him. She wet the washcloth and pressed it to his mouth. He sucked thirstily at it, so she continued to wet and press until he turned away.

Picking up the cup and spoon and taking the cloth with her to rinse it out, Samantha tucked the lightweight blanket under his chin, put a small log on the fire, and left him.

Using the hot water from the small pan, she washed their dishes and wiped the counter and table. Under the sink, she found an enamel pan to put water on to boil for sterilizing the washcloth.

"Come on, Hannibal," she said as she finished her cleaning. "Let's go take a look around outside."

Reluctantly the wrinkles collected themselves, then she shook and followed her outside the cabin. The sun had dropped behind the mountain, bringing chilled air to make her shiver as she stood taking in their complete isolation.

A few hundred yards from the cabin she could see where the fire had burned and the firebreak they had been digging when the accident occurred. No burn patients came through Young, but they were not equipped to treat burns as well as hospitals in Tacoma or Seattle. Broken, jagged bones were complicated enough, and she was deeply thankful Mr. Jordan had no burns for her to contend with.

At the edge of the thick forest, Samantha turned to look for Hannibal only to discover her right on her heels. "Don't go hunting in those trees, lady, and get lost. If you get that skin hung on a bush, you'll never get loose, and I'd never find you with the leaves turning. You'd blend right into the golden leaves." She smiled at the ugly dog who blinked her pointed eyes at her, shaking her head as they went back inside the cabin.

Taking a thermometer from the black bag, she stuck it in the boiling water, shook it down, and went into the bedroom. Mr. Jordan was asleep and as relaxed as harness and her cloth ties would allow him. Easing the thermometer between his parted lips, she slipped her fingers beneath the wrist of the hand bound by the sling bandage on his dislocated shoulder. Long fingers flexed a little and were still as she counted his pulse, strong and steady. A moment later, she removed the thermometer, pleased to see that his temperature was only a fraction over one hundred degrees. She shifted the huge body a fraction and let the harness down an inch. He groaned and mumbled.

"It's okay," she whispered. "Everything's okay."

Samantha stirred the low fire in the fireplace and placed another log on it, going back into the kitchen to get blankets from the small bunk. Fixing a thick pallet of blankets near the fire, she placed her sleeping bag on top of it. It was best she be near the patient while he was only semiconscious.

Leaving the door open, she returned to the kitchen, looking for the paperback novel in her bag, one she had started weeks ago and never had time to finish. Now would be a good time to find out who done it—and why.

Settling herself at the table in one of the small chairs, Samantha tried to relax but was uncomfortable. As she started to rise, she found her feet trapped beneath a warm bundle of wrinkles.

"For goodness sake, Hannibal," she said impatiently, looking down at the animal. Suddenly she laughed aloud. "You make a great foot warmer, but ten to one, when I need you, you'll decide not to be available."

"Sam," a voice bellowed from the next room.

Samantha was big, but she could move and was by his side in an instant. He stared with glazed eyes at her as she bent over him. He had torn the strips from his good arm and pulled the harness half off the track, hanging suspended, half on the bed and half off, tangled sheets barely covering him.

Without a word she braced herself and shoved, holding the harness with her left hand, carefully supporting his injured shoulder with the other.

"Try to help me," she told him, not sure if he understood what she said.

He relaxed a little, allowing her to move his leg onto the bed, but a big hand held onto her arm as she struggled.

"Lie back," she said, and with her help, he eased his head back to the pillow.

Reaching upward, she swung most of her weight on the harness until she could slip the track back to fit under it. Breathing hard, she let herself back down on the heels of her feet, looking into his wide-open eyes.

"You're pretty," he said just before he closed his eyes.

Samantha smiled down into the bearded face, the only features plainly visible to her being the finely molded mouth and bushy brows. The high forehead was deeply tanned, as were his hands.

He lay still as she moved away from him, drawing deep breaths to steady her nerves after that frantic exertion.

"Pretty?" she said to the sleeping giant. "At least you don't say I look like Ann-Margret." She straightened the sheet over him and pulled the light blanket up. The night would be much chillier even though she would keep both the fires going all night.

With one more look toward her patient, she headed for the back door. Hannibal was draped altogether near the bedroom door, watching the treatment her master was receiving.

"Come on," she told her. "We need to bring in more wood." The dog unfolded herself and was at Samantha's heels as she stood looking at the cords of wood stacked neatly by the cabin. The sun dropped behind the mountains and darkness came quickly as Samantha gathered an armload of wood to take inside. Four trips later, she decided it was enough for both fires.

Making sure the chain locks were attached to both doors, she checked the stove to see that the fire was safely contained, added more water to the pot she had put there, and pulled the chain to turn out the single light bulb.

"It's been a long time since I had sleep, Hannibal, and since I don't know your master's sleeping habits, I'm going to get what I can now. Coming?"

Light from the fireplace in the next room came through the open door, and she could see well enough not to stumble over the few furnishings. Paul Bunyan, alias Nicholas Jordan, lay still, his face turned away from her. Samantha touched his forehead and slid her fingers around his wrist to check his pulse. No problem there. As her eyes went over the intricate workings of the harnesses, she nodded. With long-practiced movements, she shifted his body, moving the uninjured arm back and forth before she put it alongside his body. He didn't stir.

Taking the lotion, she began the massage necessary to confined bed patients and, with a last adjustment to the sling on his injured shoulder, she left him to begin undressing near the fire. Hannibal watched from the corner of Samantha's makeshift bed.

"Squatter's rights?" she inquired and received a long sigh in answer.

The long flannel gown she had thrown in her suitcase at the last moment would feel good tonight, and the velour robe wouldn't be out of place either. Standing near the fire, she pulled the gown over her head, wrapped the robe around her, then sat near Hannibal.

"Isn't this romantic?" she asked the sleeping animal. "Firelight, a handsome man, and man's best friend. What more could I ask?" She grinned to herself and unzipped the sleeping bag to insert her body into it, leaving it open in case she had to exit in a hurry during the night.

Now that she had relaxed, exhaustion put off all day caught up with her, and she was soon fast asleep. Hannibal got up and moved closer, her wrinkled face near that of the woman who cared for her master. The dog, too, was asleep as she exhaled a long sigh.

A loud noise startled her, and Samantha sat up, rubbing her eyes, instantly awake now that she had a patient to look after. Her eyes became accustomed to the dimness of the room, lit only by the low fire, and widened as she saw Nicholas Jordan sitting up on the bunk.

"Holy cow," she muttered and moved quickly. The man hung from the harness, pulling it from the track again, his good leg strained against the strips she had fastened there. The noise that woke her was the result of his pillow being flung with such force that the small chair splintered as it was slammed into the log wall of the cabin.

Her hands were gentle even as she used the strength

in her arms to push him down, reaching to pull his leg closer to his body. Checking the harness, she found there was no breakage, but she couldn't get it back on the track until she could get him to lie down.

"Come on," she pleaded. "Lie down. I'll get your pillow." She forced him down by pressing on the right side of his chest away from the shoulder restrained by the sling. Eyes closed, Nicholas Jordan was breathing hard with low mutterings. Samantha left him to retrieve the pillow and came back to slide it beneath the shaggy head. It took five minutes of adjusting and turning before she could retrack the harness and tie the strips again, this time across his wide body to the other side of the bunk.

His face was flushed and she automatically checked his pulse to find it racing. In the bag she had brought from the kitchen, she found the medication, quickly reread the instructions on the bottle, and filled the needle. Thankful for his stillness, she gave him the shot and went for the washcloth to bathe his face, placing the opened medicine in the refrigerator as she went.

After several minutes of bathing and massaging, she checked his pulse to find it had quieted a little. Going to the foot of the bunk, she ran experienced fingers beneath the bandages, feeling for abnormal swelling. There was none and Samantha breathed a sigh of relief. Working along the badly broken leg, she checked for any other signs of trouble. At his hipbone, she pressed lightly and he moaned.

"All I can say is your Dr. Knight better find his way back here with someone to get you where you can be cared for better than I can do." A sudden anger at whoever's idea it was to leave him went through her. "He could be crippled for life if he doesn't get the proper treatment in time."

Even so, they were right in not moving him more than necessary without proper transportation, thereby preventing further damage to the leg.

"I'll say one thing: You go all out to do it right when you do it, mister. Aside from killing yourself, you do a great job of trying to become a cripple."

Leaving her patient quiet for the time being, she picked up the pieces of the chair to put them by the fireplace to use as kindling. It had lost its use as a chair.

Through all her concentrated attention on Nicholas Jordan, Samantha had forgotten Hannibal. She looked around to find the dog near her master's head, her expression one of extreme sadness—not that she could look any other way.

Hands on her wide hips, Samantha watched the two of them a moment, shaking her head. "I should write a book," she said aloud. "Either fantasy or science fiction would fit this situation."

It was three o'clock in the morning and the fire had burned down to red embers, so Samantha put several thin splinters from the destroyed chair on them and a log on top of that. In moments small flames licked around the log, and she turned to crawl back into the sleeping bag after one more look at her patient. He was quiet for now, and Hannibal lay nearby, head on her paws.

In the flickering light from the fire, she stared at the ceiling of split logs. It was a hunter's cabin, built tightly to withstand cold, wind, and rain; the Cascade Mountains were endowed with plenty of all three through the span of a year. If not filled with modern inventions, it was utilitarian.

Sounds from the bunk woke her, and she moved quickly to reach it. The room was chilly and the blanket had slid away from the broad shoulders of Nicholas Jordan. He was shivering as she covered him and touched his cheek to find it cool. Moving back to her sleeping bag, Samantha picked up the heavy robe she had discarded and went back to wrap him in its warmth. As she tucked it over his chest, she saw his blue eyes open wide.

"Good morning, Mr. Jordan," she said, smiling at him.

He stared at her, and she decided he wasn't fully awake and turned to put more wood on the fire. Even though she was certain the temperature hadn't dropped to freezing, it was too cool to allow either fire to go out. "Better pep up the one in the kitchen, too."

"What the hell's going on?" the voice from the bunk demanded.

"Welcome to reality," she said as she moved to stand beside him. Hannibal, hearing her master's voice, reared up on hind legs and put her forelegs on the arm tied to the side of the bunk.

Nicholas Jordan ignored Samantha and looked at the dog, grinning to show white teeth beneath the shaggy beard. "A familiar face, at least," he said, trying to free his arm. He glared at Samantha.

"Take these damned ropes off me," he demanded.

"Will you behave if I do?"

"Behave?"

"Yes, you know, not fight with me or try to maul me; that type of behave."

He grinned. "I won't fight. Mauling sounds more to my liking."

Ignoring his sassy comment, she touched his forehead. "How do you feel?"

The grin faded. "Like I've been roped and tied. Every bone in me hurts." He looked down at his body. "The last thing I remember is that damned tractor rearing up like a wild bronco."

"You're rather the worse for wear, that's for sure." Samantha told him what little she knew about the accident and watched as realization hit him.

"You mean I'll probably be crippled for life?" Anger darkened the blue eyes, and he gave her a look that blamed her for the entire problem. "You mean I'm stuck here in this cabin with just you to look out for me?"

"That's right, Mr. Jordan. Just me. And I might add a reluctant just me. I was commandeered for the job because I was the next best thing to the male nurse they couldn't find." Sudden resentment at being assigned the ungrateful patient went through her.

His ominous glance went over her, standing there in her flannel gown that might look cute on some small female but served only to make her look twice as wide as she was.

He grunted. "Just wait till I get hold of Foster. It must be his doings." He strained at the ties holding him, looking volumes at her. "Well, you're definitely not male," he acknowledged, "whatever else you might be."

Samantha didn't answer him because if she had, she'd have hit him, tied up and defenseless or not. Turning away, she reached to the foot of the bed and handed him the bedpan. "You probably need this."

He stared in astonishment. "I'm not using that damned thing," he said. "I'll go to the bathroom."

"Really?" she asked. "You're a big man, Mr. Jordan, but I feel inclined to disagree that you can take bunk and all to the back porch, even if you could walk alone. In the first place, you couldn't get it through that door." She smirked at him, ignoring the thundering frown on his face.

She placed the bedpan within his reach and untied the knots from the strips holding his good arm. He flexed it and reached to rub the injured shoulder, wincing as he did so.

Sympathy took the place of her little spurt of anger and she said, "I'll loosen all the bandages and massage you after breakfast. That will help your circulation and lessen the throbbing."

"How do you know it throbs?" he asked. "How many times have you been strung up like this?"

"Never, but I've been around people like you." She smiled. "Never in this exact situation, I must admit." She turned. "I'll start breakfast and be back for that."

Samantha turned away, ignoring his suggestion as to what she could do with the bedpan, and went into the kitchen. The stove was barely warm, and it took a few minutes to get the fire going again.

In the pantry she found canned meat and a few minutes later, the smell of frying bacon filled the small room.

"Sam!" The call from the adjoining room could only be described as a bellow coming from an injured bear, and Samantha grinned to herself as she went to retrieve the bedpan. Without looking at him, she took it and went through the kitchen onto the back porch and into the bathroom.

The air was chilly but clear, and she looked with delight at the sight of the sun peeping over the heavy foliage. If she and Leo were camping, she would be even more appreciative. Shrugging and accepting her temporary bondage, she went to check breakfast.

Gathering items she needed, she went to the bunk, handing Nicholas Jordan a cloth wet in warmed water. He wiped over his forehead and eyes, over the heavy bearded chin, returning the cloth without a word. She wiped his free hand, marveling at the bigness of it, the long fingers with well-shaped nails. The hand didn't look as though it belonged to a logger, even though it was sized for it. She picked up the other hand that was bound closely to his chest, separating the fingers to wipe them. They were only slightly swollen, and she pressed the flesh gently.

"Does that hurt?" she asked.

"No," was his short answer.

"Good. As soon as we eat, I'll take that bandage off and take a look at your shoulder." She smiled down at him. He looked very tired. "You'll be able to rest better when we can make that smaller, and you can at least move your shoulder a little bit."

A few minutes later, she returned with a plate of

steaming food and looked around for a place to sit, re-membered the destroyed chair she had used on the fire, and returned to the kitchen to haul one of the small ones from the table with her.

He watched every move she made, and when she sat by him, he struggled to sit up. "It would be better if you let me feed you, Mr. Jordan," she said, reading his mind.

"I can do it," he said.

Without answering, she pushed the chair near the bed, placing the plate on it and handed him a fork. "Would you like some orange juice?"

"Yes."

Returning with a small plastic glass, she stood watching as he tried unsuccessfully to feed himself, finally taking the fork from him and sitting down to do it for him. He made no objection this time.

After only a few bites he shook his head, took the glass from her, and downed the juice in one swallow. Samantha didn't insist he eat any more, preferring him to eat often rather than force him. Back in the kitchen, she ate her breakfast, washed their dishes, and let Hannibal in from her brief sortie to the edge of the woods. She returned to her master's bedside and flopped in a golden pile.

Samantha joined them. "Are you in pain, Mr. Jordan?" she asked, looking down at the still figure.

Weariness was in the movement required to open his eyes, but he somehow managed to glare. "I hurt like hell," he informed her.

"Where?"

"All over."

She opened the black medical bag and removed two bottles, reading the labels before removing one capsule from each. Then she handed them to him with a glass of water.

"Take both of these, and I'll give you a shot to relieve some of the soreness." She went toward the kitchen to get the bottle of medicine from the refrigerator.

He held out the glass to her as she came back to the bed and looked from the needle to her as she paused. Samantha smiled at the look on his face and said, "It will be better for you if I give it to you in your hip. It works faster that way."

Muttering what she took to be uncomplimentary instructions, Nicholas Jordan turned his head as she lifted the sheet and gave him the shot in his good hip. He didn't flinch even though the shot was heavy and must have been, at the least, uncomfortable.

In the kitchen she used her makeshift method of sterilizing all utensils, set everything aside to be ready for usage again, and went back to her patient. His eyes were closed, but the big fist on the injured arm opened and closed.

"Let me adjust the bandage and sling and move you around some, Mr. Jordan," she said. "Then you can go to sleep."

The baleful glare wasn't very forceful, and she proceeded to do what she could to move him into a different position.

"Did anyone else get hurt?" he asked.

"Dr. Knight mentioned four more who were injured, but I don't know how badly. He said you had just about completed the firebreak when the accident happened. The tractor hit a hidden tree trunk and turned over on you, but they were able to contain the fire."

"Stupid campers," he grumbled. "They shouldn't be allowed in here when it's as dry as it's been this fall."

"All campers are not careless, Mr. Jordan. I happen to do a lot of it, and I've never caused a fire. Surely you wouldn't punish all of us for a few who make mistakes."

His gaze went over her. She had changed into the navy pants and sweater and brushed her short blond hair into a neat frame for her face. The brisk air outside had brought the color to her fair skin, accenting the natural pale rose of her full lips.

"You like to camp? Do you fish?"

"I like to camp; I don't care to fish. I like to walk out where there are few people and lots of forest folks." Her fingers on his pulse, Samantha touched his forehead with her other hand and slipped the thermometer into his mouth as he started to speak again.

"That's better," she said, removing and checking the thermometer. "Now all we have to do is get your bones knitting back right, and you'll be on your way."

When he didn't answer, she looked to see his eyes were closed. Taking her robe from around his chest, she straightened the sheet and blanket and went to put another log on the low fire. It was comfortable in the room.

With one last glance at the sleeping man, she left the room, and as she closed the door, Hannibal came through on her heels, stopping just outside the room.

"Oh, he's going to be okay, Hannibal," she told her. "He isn't going to leave you of his own accord for quite a while, so you can be content right here with me." As the dog continued to look up at her, she went on, "No, you don't get anything to eat until tonight."

Ignoring the pleading in the pagoda-shaped eyes, Samantha went about cleaning the small room, sterilized the syringes she had used, and put another pot of water on to boil. She grinned, anticipating the bellow when she approached Nicholas Jordan to bathe him after his nap.

"Let's go outside and look around, Hannibal," she said, and the dog reluctantly moved her wrinkles to join her.

The sun was topping the trees and morning mist rose a few feet from the damp earth. The burned smell was still strong enough to irritate her nose, and she sneezed. She could almost agree with Nicholas Jordan that campers not be allowed in the forest, but she enjoyed her treks and camping almost all year long, keeping to the lower elevations during the winter, and she didn't want to be barred from a hobby she loved.

"This area is closed during the winter," she said to the disinterested dog. "Someone had better remember that we're up here before they close it off until next spring." She thought about it a moment and smiled. "I don't know. With the daily wage they're paying me, maybe I should hope they'd leave us here until next summer, and I could retire."

Clustered around the space where the cabin sat were a few towering ponderosa pines, plus spindly oaks and birches intermingled with a large redwood here and there. They were not the usual trees that made up raw material necessary for profitable lumbering, the main reason campers were allowed in the area. She supposed that Nicholas Jordan, along with the other men, had been commandeered from their jobs to fight the fire.

Samantha set off at a brisk pace, circling the edge of the trees, a reluctant Hannibal beside her. Fifteen minutes later they were back at the door, the dog panting.

"You're in terrible shape, Hannibal," she said. "Not only do you need to go on a diet, but exercise should be a daily regimen for you, although it doesn't seem to help me one way or the other." She looked down at the dog. "Whether I starve myself or walk a hundred miles, I never lose any weight." She sighed. "Perhaps we're both hopeless cases."

The kitchen was pleasantly warm, and she left the back door open for a few minutes as she went into the next room to check on Nicholas Jordan. He moved restlessly, and she picked up his hand to check the pulse. It was a little rapid but nothing to worry about at the moment. His forehead was cool to her touch.

"Sam," he murmured and the big hand closed over hers. She was suddenly looking into wide-open, electric-blue eyes.

"Do you hurt?"

"No, but I'm tired." He didn't release her hand, and she used her other one to check the track holding the injured leg immobile.

"Let go, Mr. Jordan," she told him. "I need to loosen this a little."

Samantha stretched over him, her arm supporting

his leg as she adjusted the pulley, and grunted. "This bunk wasn't designed for people with broken legs," she said, straining to reach the opposite side.

"If the owners had suspected that I'd break all my bones and you'd have to stay here alone with me, I'm sure they'd have put it in the center of the room," he said.

She let herself down on her feet slowly, looking into his face to see if she could read the expression in his voice. His hand moved gently over her breast, and she drew in a swift breath, taking a step backward.

He smiled. "I can't take advantage of you, Sam, but I won't put up much of a fight if you decide to take advantage of me."

Amorous patients were only one of the hazards of nursing, and Samantha had learned to sidestep. The fact that she wasn't slim and trim didn't deter the handyman when he was confined.

"Get well first," she told him, "then meet me on even ground. I wouldn't want to use unfair tactics on a helpless patient." She moved closer to the bunk to un-wrap the bandaged left shoulder. "But if you don't let me change this bandage without a wrestling match, I'll accidentally fall on you and, believe me, if you think the tractor was heavy, that will really get your attention."

He grinned, his eyes going over her buxom figure as she worked, but he made no attempt to touch her again, causing her to wonder why she felt breathless all of a sudden. She could still feel the touch of his fingers on her breast as she replaced the awkward bandage with a smaller one, and when she finished, she went into the kitchen, shaking her head at the sensation still spreading through her at the burly man's unexpected caress.

He was different; maybe that was the reason he stirred her. There was no ring on his left hand, but she wasn't sure men wore wedding rings anymore. Anyway, he was helpless. *Not by a long shot is he helpless,* she corrected herself, thinking of the huge hands, the self-assured grin teasing her even when she knew he was in pain.

Taking a pan of hot water, soap, towel, and washcloth with her as she returned to the bedroom, Samantha placed them on the small table by the bunk. He watched silently as she began to bathe him and made no more unexpected moves during the time it took her to complete his bath. Neither of them spoke, but heat came unexpectedly to her face. She turned away from him so he couldn't see her discomfort, trying to remember the last time she had been embarrassed by bathing a male patient.

Giving herself a hardy mental shake, she rewrapped his shoulder, her long fingers probing the dislocated area. Dr. Knight had done a fabulous job of forcing the bones back into the right position, and the splint could be removed in a few days. The leg, however, was a different story.

"You have beautiful hands, Sam."

"Thank you, Mr. Jordan."

"How long do you think we'll be here like this?"

She shook her head. "Dr. Knight assured me he'd be back in a few days, and maybe by then he can tell when you can be moved without doing any harm."

The shaggy head turned on the pillow, blue eyes following the pulley that held his leg and hip immobile. He closed his eyes. "Then you'd better call me Nick. Every time you say 'Mr. Jordan,' I think you're talking to Foster."

"Who's Foster?" she asked, remembering his reference to the name once before.

"My dad." His eyes opened suddenly and he grinned. "I like your name, Sam; it suits you."

She winced at the masculinity of the name. "My name is Samantha," she reminded him firmly.

"Sounds too formal." He nodded with satisfaction, closing his eyes again. "Sam," he said and turned his face away from her.

Chapter Four

Samantha made another quick check of the pantry and the wood stacked at the back of the cabin. Hannibal at her heels, she walked with long strides around the clearing and into the trees to the edge of the burned-out area, wincing when she saw the gouges in the earth where the tractor had overturned.

Nicholas Jordan suffered dangerous injuries that would require meticulous care and a long convalescence to heal correctly and prevent the broken leg from being shorter than the uninjured one. It would be a long, long time before he'd be able to return to logging—or any job where he would have to do a lot of walking or lifting.

"He'll be a difficult patient, Hannibal," she said to the dog sitting by her foot. "He'll try us one and all, I'm positive, so let's hope Dr. Knight comes through with some help before it comes to a wrestling match between us."

The down jacket she wore kept her warm despite wind blowing through the thick trees. She stood there, daydreaming in the clean, crisp air that still carried the faint smell of charred timber.

Benjy would be giving the hospital staff fits, slipping from his supports and scooting down the hall in search of "Bridges." Leo would be on one of a number of emergencies that occurred during the course of the day at Young. Ida Vincent might be wondering what was happening with her pseudomale nurse detailed into the wilderness at the demand of some faraway executive of a lumber company.

Perhaps Myers Reston would have a few minutes' attack of conscience for having done her out of her coveted days off after the grueling eleven-to-seven shift, but she doubted it. He had performed his duty the way a competent administrative director should, and that was that.

A sudden dimness made her look up at the sky to see black clouds moving in over the tops of the highest trees, obscuring the sun. Combined with the accompanying winds, they could mean trouble.

Samantha frowned. "Don't get fickle with me," she said aloud to the weather. "More problems I don't need. Give me a few days to get help and maybe even a little more advice about what to do with Mr. Jordan."

Nick, he had said to call him. Nicholas had a more romantic sound to it, she thought again, aware that the warmth in her cheeks was moving throughout her body. Samantha turned impatiently toward the cabin, glancing once more at the darkening sky. She stopped at the stacks of wood and gathered an armful to deposit in the kitchen. Hannibal walked with what dignity she could muster into her master's room and dropped altogether near the bunk.

Samantha stepped to the door of the next room and looked at the still figure before turning to go to the pantry in search of something she could fix for their lunch.

Selecting a can of clear soup, she moved some of the items until she found a can of sliced peaches and an unopened box of Minute Rice. She prepared the meal, sufficient though not too original, and a few minutes later made her way into the bedroom, placing the dishes on the table by the bed. Nicholas Jordan hadn't moved.

She touched his forehead to find it cool; fingers on his pulse counted it normal. She let out a relieved breath: Her patient was on his way to recovery, barring unforeseen complications. Crossing her fingers, she sent an inward plea to Dr. Knight not to be too long in returning and looked back into the face of her patient to meet his wide-open stare.

"Hungry?" she asked.

"Got any steak?"

"Next best thing," she told him. "Hot soup with rice and a delicious dessert of canned peaches."

He grimaced. "I guess I'm still being hand-fed?"

"Any other suggestions?"

"Yes," he said, firm lips tightening. "But I don't think I'd better make them since I'm still at your mercy."

"As long as you remember that, Nicholas." She smiled. "You and I will get along just fine."

"I won't always be this helpless," he threatened.

"Nor will I always be nearby," she answered. "Now stop talking so I can get some food into you."

The feeding continued in silence until she raised the glass to his lips. "What's that?" he demanded.

"Milk."

A dangerous glint came into his eyes, turning them dark. "Not on your life will I drink that powdered stuff. Didn't they leave any beer in the refrigerator?"

"You couldn't have it even if they did, which they didn't," she said. "Besides, this doesn't taste like regular powdered milk. I doctored it up to make it easier to drink. Try it."

He shook his head, glaring, but she put the plate and fork down and stood so that she could lift the glass to his mouth.

"Come on, Nicholas. Don't try my patience any more than you have already."

A cunning look came into the blue eyes. "Get just a little closer, Sam, and I'll show you how impatient I can be."

"And I'll dump this glass of milk right down your belly."

They glared at each other, blue eyes staring into hazel that refused to look away from him even though she was beginning to feel electric pinpoints all the way down into her serviceable oxfords. She stiffened, refusing to back away from him. He almost smiled as he relented with a slight nod, leaning toward the glass just a tiny bit.

Sliding her left hand under his neck, Samantha lifted his head, thick hair falling long enough to cover her wrist and sending an errant flash of warmth all along her arm. She bit her lip as she met the teasing eyes, but held the glass to his mouth until he took a sip from it, helping balance it with his right hand.

She moved it away until he swallowed, closing his eyes tightly and pressing his lips together. He licked his lips and the heavy lashes lifted again.

His voice showed surprise. "You're right; that isn't too bad. What did you do to it?"

"My secret," she said and continued with her feeding, avoiding as much as possible meeting the directness of his glance.

When she finished giving him the peaches, he sighed and lay back on the pillow. The small amount of effort had tired him out completely. She wiped his face.

"Do you have a comb or brush?" she asked, smoothing the shaggy hair away from his forehead, straightening the covers, and checking the harness again.

He shook his head. "I didn't bring anything with me here since I was only going to be in the area a couple of hours." Eyes closed, he sounded weary. "The best laid plans of mice and men," he murmured.

"I know what you mean," she agreed, taking the dishes and moving to the kitchen.

"Sam?"

She turned. "Yes, Nicholas?"

His eyes were only half open, but he grinned. "I'm glad you're here. I like having a private nurse, a real private nurse I don't have to share with anyone." Lashes settled against his cheek, and smiling, she left him to go to her cleanup duties.

Surprisingly Samantha found plenty to occupy her, so the afternoon went by in a hurry. Outside the wind had risen and the clouds were darker and hung lower over the trees. She brought in several armfuls of wood and stacked some in each room, checking Nicholas every few minutes as he slept the afternoon away.

"Just like a baby," she said to Hannibal. "He and I are going to have some words if he gets his days and nights mixed and decides to stay awake all night." The dog yawned with huge gaping jaws and ignored her comments.

"Sam!" The familiar bellow brought her around from her survey of the threatening weather, and she hurried into the bedroom.

"Yes, Nicholas?" she asked, relieved to see him lying down instead of hanging from the straps.

He gave her his now-famous glare. "I need that damned instrument of torture," he said.

Instant recognition of the description of the bedpan brought a smile to her mouth, and she turned without a word to get it for him. She was waiting just outside the door for his second yell and hurried to relieve him. Her sympathy was with anyone who had to use the bedpan, and she removed it quickly and left him to take care of what had to be done, going back to plump his pillow and straighten the bedclothes around him. With the medicated lotion, Samantha massaged him in rhythmic movements long-practiced on her bedridden patients.

As she half turned him to reach his back, he murmured, "That feels good."

"Do you have pain in the shoulder?"

"No, but my hip feels like somebody is beating it with a hammer."

"It will for a few days," she told him. "I'm sorry. As

soon as they can move you, more can be done to relieve the pressure without damaging it. I can only do so much shifting without doing some harm.''

He was quiet for a moment as she worked the lotion into his leg. ''What are the chances of my leg being normal again?''

She shook her head. ''The fractures are complex and it will take a long time and a lot of therapy, but with the new treatments and equipment they have now, your chances are very good.'' She stood up and capped the bottle of lotion. ''The sooner they get you into a good orthopedic center, the better your chances.''

Anger darkened his features as much as she could see beneath the beard. ''I don't care to be a cripple the rest of my life.''

''You're lucky to be alive, Nicholas.''

''That's what I want to be—alive, not crippled for life.''

She looked down at him. ''Alive, you have a chance. Dead, you don't.''

''In addition to being Florence Nightingale, I suppose you're a psychologist, too?''

''Out here I'm all you have, so don't knock it,'' she said, turning to leave the room.

''Yeah,'' he said, the teasing back in his voice. ''They could have found that male nurse.''

She flipped a dark look at him over her shoulder and went to heat dinner.

He ate silently this time, watching her as she avoided meeting his gaze directly. Concentrating on making her insides behave at his closeness, Samantha was able to keep the telltale color from her face.

He took the washcloth from her hand and wiped his mouth. "What do you and Hannibal eat if you feed me all the gourmet items on the menu?"

"As you know, Hannibal eats anything that doesn't run from her, and I'll manage with leftover tidbits from the master's dinner."

"When I get out of here, remind me that I owe you a steak dinner at the best restaurant in Seattle," he said.

"That's a long ways from Yakima," she told him, smiling. "But, thanks anyway. A strenuous diet won't hurt anything but my feelings."

His blue gaze went over her. "I like women who look like they know how to eat," he said.

She nodded. "I can imagine your well-fed girl friends, Nicholas."

"You can? How?" He straightened on the pillow.

Assuming a thoughtful pose, she gave him her description. "Tall, perhaps five feet seven or eight inches, weighing maybe one hundred ten pounds. Sultry dark eyes, black hair as a foil for your blondeness. Dresses elegantly... and worships Nicholas Jordan."

His laugh rang out as deep as his bellow, and a delicious thrill went through her at the sound. "What if I told you she was fat and forty?"

"Is she?"

Continuing to smile at her, he shook his head. "No, as a matter of fact you're quite close in your description, but she's as tall as you and weighs one hundred and twenty-five pounds."

She groaned, shaking her head. "So rub it in, you monster."

Measure of Love

The smile left his face. "You wouldn't look good that thin, Sam."

"I don't have to worry about it, Nicholas," she said, keeping her voice carefully light. After straightening his covers, she left him to get dinner for Hannibal, who waited patiently as Samantha opened the can for her and immediately disposed of the contents. She refilled the dish with burger bits and reheated some dinner for herself.

Finishing her kitchen cleanup duties, she peeked into the bedroom to see Nicholas with eyes closed, lying quietly as she left him, and went to find her book. She stopped by the small window to look outside, feeling a moment of disquiet as she watched the trees bending in the wind that had once again picked up out of the northeast. It was getting dark in a hurry, a bad habit of this part of the country in mid-October, especially areas with plenty of trees around.

She frowned, thinking about the remark Nicholas made about careless campers, knowing he was partly right. Some people, campers or not, were thoughtless when it came to life and limb of others, and animals didn't register in their minds as being anything to worry about. Watching the shifting shadows deepen, she remembered Leo's concentration on keeping their fire under control, making absolutely sure it was out before they left.

Nodding to herself and smiling as she thought of him, she decided Leo was one of the best to go camping with and she missed him. By the time she returned to civilization, it would be too late for other than a couple of weekend ventures unless they went south near the Oregon border where the weather remained mild longer than up at this elevation.

Blackness engulfed the outside, and she turned back to look for Hannibal. The dog wasn't in the room with her, and she stepped back to the other door to see her lying near the bunk where Nicholas slept.

"Good," Samantha mumbled to herself. They would keep each other company for a while and let her relax.

Her novel had reached the interesting part where the heroine was just about to find out who was trying to kidnap her when the bellow came from the next room.

"Sam!"

The book tumbled from her lap as she hurried to see what calamity had befallen her charge, surprised to see him lying in the same position she had left him. Hannibal stood with big paws planted firmly on his chest.

Satisfied that nothing terrible was happening to either of them, she stood with hands on her hips. "What does the master need? He has his faithful animal to protect him and looks fairly comfortable, so what's his problem?"

He didn't glare at her this time but smiled like a little boy caught stealing from the cookie jar. His teeth were white beneath the heavy beard.

"I don't suppose you have an extra toothbrush? My mouth feels like someone fertilized their garden in it."

"I'll see what I can do. Just don't frighten me with that Tarzan yell so often. I always think of the awful things that can happen to you, and my heart will only take so much of the shock." She patted Hannibal on her thick shoulder, gently urging her paws from her master's chest.

"She isn't hurting me," he said. He eyed the dog affectionately. "Isn't she a beauty?"

"Beauty?" Samantha echoed in astonishment, shaking her head. "I'm not much of an authority on dogs, but to my twenty-twenty vision she's about the ugliest critter I've ever seen."

"How can you say that? She's only one of less than a hundred of her kind in the United States and the best of her breed."

"And what, in the name of St. Helens, is that?" she asked, unimpressed by his statistics.

"She's a Shar-pei, originally from China. Affluent women at one time considered it a real status symbol to have a coat made from their skin."

Samantha shuddered. "How horrible!" Her fingers caressed the dog and became lost in the heavy rolls of skin and hair she encountered. Hannibal turned to look at her, pointed eyes accepting her petting as her due. Her five o'clock shadowed muzzle separated as she covered Samantha's hand with a loving slurp.

She withdrew her hand from the dog. "I'll see about that toothbrush," she said and left master and animal to their mutual admiration society.

Her suitcase had been shoved into a corner, and she opened the side pocket to rummage for the cases she always kept there, coming up with a yellow plastic holder. She shook it. Sure enough, it held a new toothbrush, just as she knew it would. One of her better habits: carrying extra toothbrushes no matter where she went.

With toothpaste and a plastic glass from the cabinet, she took her makeshift receptacle into the bedroom, nudging Hannibal aside as she bent over the bunk.

Nicholas opened his eyes, and she felt the now-familiar tingle go through her as he treated her to the full benefit of his intense blue-eyed stare.

Be still, my heart, Samantha told her insides. He's only a job. A job with a skinny, gorgeous girl friend somewhere back in civilization.

She placed the items on the table and turned to look over the trussed-up figure, her professional gaze judging what could be done at the moment.

Looking back at him, she said, "Let me loosen the pulley to give me more room to maneuver, and I can massage you better before I tighten it again. Then you can brush your teeth."

Feeling somewhat as she did with Benjy, she noticed the tiredness around his eyes, the dark circles not hidden by the beard. He was probably in a lot of pain, but being the he-man he was, he refused to tell her.

She made an impatient sound. "Do you hurt anywhere?"

This time he glared. "What the hell do you think? You're supposed to know about things like this." He moved the hand trussed up with the sling on his shoulder and grimaced.

Refusing to be intimidated into sympathizing with him, Samantha took the hand and straightened out the fingers, noticing that her hands were lost beneath his. Kneading gently but firmly, she moved from his fingers down his wrist as far as she could go toward his elbow, using her fingers to probe as she went back and forth on his arm.

He sighed. "Feels nice." The big hand turned and captured hers with a strength that belied the fact that any movement must be painful to him. "I love your hands, Sam. You must hear that a lot in your job."

"Yes," she said. It was true. There had been many comments on her lovely hands, healing hands. It was a compliment she accepted, since she never heard anyone talk about her eye-stopping figure.

"Let go, Nicholas," she told him, and when he complied with her request, she reached upward to loosen the pulley holding his injured leg. Working her way downward, she released a little at a time until she had him where she could work some lotion into all the exposed area, noting with satisfaction there was no swelling in his foot.

He lay quietly as she worked on the huge foot, rubbing and pressing into the skin around his ankle that had escaped being broken. She didn't see how any part of him had been so lucky, but he should be thankful no anklebones had been crushed. They healed so slowly, and most patients got in so much of a hurry to walk that reinjury of those bones was frequently the cause of permanent damage.

Finishing with his bad side, Samantha turned to work her way down his right side, adjusting the towel to cover him as she went, keeping her face turned carefully away from his bright-eyed stare. The silence grew louder and louder, but she kept her mind on her professional job and finished without speaking, recapping the lotion bottle to set it aside.

"Now, the teeth," she told him, smiling as she loaded the brush with paste and placed it in his uninjured hand. While he performed that light duty, she put wood on the fire, stirring the red-hot coals to flames.

Going back to the bedside, she took the brush and waited as he rinsed his mouth.

"Better?"

Nicholas nodded. "Lots." With a tired groan, he relaxed against the pillow.

When she went back to the bed, she took the thermometer and shot preparations. He shook his head. "I don't need that anymore."

"You get it anyway; it's included in your bill," she said.

Resigned to the inevitable, he turned his head so she could slip the thermometer into his mouth, her fingers on his pulse.

"If it's too fast, it's because of you," he told her, eyes glinting mischievously.

Shades of Benjy, Samantha thought. "Shut up so I can get an accurate reading on your temperature." Three quiet minutes later, she recorded a ninety-nine-degree temperature and normal pulse rate.

"Now the shot," she said and lifted the sheet to inject the medicine into his hip. Nicholas grinned as her face colored, and she slapped an alcohol-soaked cotton ball a little harder than necessary on the spot where she withdrew the needle.

Taking the capsules she had placed on the table, she popped them into his mouth and handed him a glass of water. As he swallowed and returned the glass to her, she plumped his pillow, pulling the sheet tightly to remove wrinkles that might make him uncomfortable.

Samantha smiled down at him. "Now go to sleep like a good boy."

"Do I get a good-night kiss?"

"No," she said shortly and turned away from him, ignoring the foolish thrill of warmth that cascaded through her body.

Boy, am I way out of line, she thought. *Much more of this and Leo and I will cease to have a platonic relationship in my own self-defense.*

She put a log on the fire, turned once more to look at Nicholas to see his eyes closed and Hannibal sprawled on the floor near him. Her sleeping bag had been dragged to the corner of the room, and she pulled it back nearer the fire, leaving it open so she could get into it easily.

In the kitchen she checked the fire in the stove, adding wood to keep it going, too, as she felt a chill in the room.

She stretched and yawned, picking up her book again, after a glance at her watch confirmed it was only nine o'clock.

Two pages later, she gave up and got ready for bed. In the firelit bedroom she looked at her two sleeping charges, undressed, slipped on the voluminous flannel gown, and went to bed.

Instantly awake at some signal, Samantha opened her eyes to look into Hannibal's anything-but-alert face, sitting up quickly as she saw the room was already light. Nicholas lay watching her and smiled when he saw she was awake.

"Why didn't you call me?" she scolded, reaching for her robe.

"You looked too comfortable, Sam," he said.

She started toward the bed, but Hannibal blocked her way, pointed eyes pleading. "Oh, all right," she said impatiently and looked at Nicholas. "Can you wait a minute until I attend to your best friend?"

Without waiting for his answer, she went to the bed and touched his forehead, cool and dry; her fingers on his pulse found it strong and normal. She let out her breath, until then unaware she had been holding it in suspense.

"I can wait," he told her.

With Hannibal leading the way, Samantha went to open the back door, looking with wary eyes at a dark, cloudy sky and trees bending before the strong wind that had changed direction from the night before and was now coming from the northwest. It could mean much-needed rain if they were in Yakima, but she had no idea what it might indicate at this elevation.

Turning to check the stove, she found only warm embers, and it took her a couple of minutes to get the fire going again. It wasn't chilly any longer but downright cold. Hurrying, she went back into the bedroom and put a log on the fire that had burned most of the night.

Nicholas hadn't moved nor made a sound as she went about quickly taking care of the minor duties necessary to their comfort.

Going to the bedside to look down at him, she asked, "How did you rest last night?"

"Not bad. If I could turn over, it would be a lot better."

Samantha nodded as she checked the harness and straightened the covers over him. "I know." Pulling the blanket up around his shoulder, she found herself close to the bearded face, with blue eyes staring straight into hers.

He smiled. "You're pretty, Sam."

Backing away from him, she waited for the hands to reach for her, but Nicholas remained still, his injured hand clenched into a mammoth fist, and she found herself thinking that whoever encountered that hunk of meat and bone was in for a jolt.

A demanding bark from the back door claimed her attention, and she went to let Hannibal in, watching the dog walk with as much dignity as her unironed appearance would allow and following her into the room where Nicholas waited for them. Without comment, she left the bedpan for him and removed it a few minutes later, all without either of them speaking.

She turned toward the kitchen. "I'll get breakfast and be right back."

Feeding sick people was a hard job—they were never quite happy with whatever was fixed and, to Samantha, the food always looked unappetizing. For that reason, she told herself, she took extra pains with her preparations of breakfast for Nicholas.

Corned beef hash with an almost-perfect egg sunny-side up in the center looked almost attractive with the toast she made in the old iron frying pan. The coffee made in the years-old percolator burned black on the bottom smelled good, but she would await further judgment until one of them tasted it.

Dropping the pain capsules into her robe pocket, she took the plate with her into the bedroom and found Nicholas staring at the ceiling. Hannibal had removed herself nearer the fire and didn't bother to acknowledge Samantha's presence in any way.

"Nicholas?" She waited for him to turn his head to look at her, his eyes going over the plate in her hand, then back to her face.

"I'm not hungry," he said.

"Don't be hard to get along with, Nicholas. We've been doing very well." His glare brought a smile to her lips. "You do that so well—I assume you've had lots of practice over the years."

"We've been very good," he mimicked her. "Who is this 'we' bit? I haven't noticed you hog-tied, depending on somebody else to do everything for you." The glare became darker. "Practiced what?"

Frowning, Samantha flattened her lips over the edge of her teeth and gave him her imitation of his expression. He fought for a moment, but the glare gradually disappeared and he laughed suddenly, a low heavy-chested laugh that brought goose bumps to her skin.

Swallowing over the sudden dryness in her throat, she said, "Now that's more like it."

After adjusting his pillow to lift him a little, she sat on the edge of the bunk to feed him. "I can hold the plate close to you if you'd like to try feeding yourself," she said.

He nodded and took the fork from her and actually managed quite well.

"I forgot the coffee," she said. "And I don't guarantee how good it is. Would you like to try it?"

"Yes," he said, resting his head on the pillow as she moved away.

Placing the plate on the table, she was quickly back

with two cups of coffee. "Do you take sugar or milk?"

"No."

"It's hot if nothing else, so be careful."

He sipped in silence before he looked back at her. "Not bad."

"Such enthusiasm for all my efforts." She clucked her tongue at him.

Meeting her glance, he smiled. "What does your family think of your being way out here in the land of Oz with a stranger—a male stranger?"

"They don't know where I am," she said.

His eyebrows went upward. "How do you get away with disappearing for days at a time and they not know?"

"My mother and sister are all I have, and they live in San Antonio and seldom know where I am."

"No husband?"

She shook her head, smiling.

"No curious boyfriend?"

"I have a friend, Nicholas, but he understands my job because he's a doctor." She took the cup from him and gave him back the plate. "He knows I'm on a private-duty case so he won't worry about me."

"He should."

She met his look. "Why would he worry about me? He knows I can take care of myself."

"Does he know your private duty is a normal male with normal male appetites?"

Color stained her cheeks, and she bit into her lips as he grinned and went on eating. Irritated at the impertinence of the man, she said sweetly, "Confine your appetite to the food I prepare, Nicholas, since you'd have a problem satisfying any other type."

His glance went over her figure, hidden beneath her oversized gown and bathrobe, before he said softly, "Oh, I don't know," and continued eating.

Samantha remained close of necessity and silently took his plate when he finished, handing him the coffee cup before she took the dishes to the kitchen. The fragrance of the coffee filled the small kitchen, and she took the old-fashioned percolator back to the bedside to refill his cup. He watched her without a word and she turned, aware that his glance followed her from the room.

Fuming at herself for her unprofessional feelings, she fixed her own breakfast and enjoyed the cup of coffee she had envied him as he drank. It was as good as she thought it would be.

After she changed her clothes and gathered the medication and lotion for Nicholas, she returned to take his cup from him, putting it in the sink with the other dishes to soak in the stove-heated water.

Taking the sterilized washcloth, she put hot water into the enamel pan and went back into the bedroom, placing the pan on the table until she replenished the wood on the fire. It was a lot warmer with the fire going well.

Turning to find Nicholas watching her, she said, "Bath time."

He didn't answer, and she proceeded with her work, neither of them speaking. Adjusting the harness and turning him slightly, she said, "I certainly hope Dr. Knight comes soon. I need someone to help me change these sheets. That would make it a lot more comfortable for you."

"The sheets don't bother me," he said.

"I know, but fresh bedclothes always help a patient's morale, I've found."

"It will take more than fresh sheets to help my morale," he said tiredly.

"Don't start that with me, Nicholas. You're in for a long haul to get back to normal, and the sooner you accept it, the better. Forgive me if my bedside manner isn't that of a placating bone specialist, but with your utmost cooperation and the best of doctors, you'll be fine. But take my word for it, you won't be walking next week."

She smiled to take some of the hardness out of her predictions, but she didn't like pussyfooting around with patients who needed to realize what they faced on the road to recovery.

"Big lumber companies have lots of money in the insurance business and their employees are taken care of, so I'm sure your boss will see that you're given competent specialists who know what to do with your type of injury." She picked up his hand, her fingers finding the strong pulse. "At least that's good luck for you."

As he opened his mouth to speak, she slipped the thermometer into his mouth and looked at her watch to count the pulse. When she removed the thermometer, she breathed a sigh of relief. It was normal, as was his pulse.

"Better, Nicholas. Much better." She handed him a capsule with a glass of water, which he swallowed without comment.

When she reached for the syringe, he shook his

head. "If I'm so much better, why do I need that?"

"It will relax you and keep your body from being so sore from lying in the bed. I can't turn you enough to relieve all the pressure." He lay still as she gave him the shot, and as she straightened, he turned his head away and closed his eyes.

For a moment Samantha was tempted to reach out and pet him, but she gave up that notion and took the various and sundry dishes and medicines back into the kitchen.

Cleanup duties performed, she checked the fires in both rooms and went to the back door, opening it to look out at the threatening sky. She frowned, not liking the looks of the clouds and changing wind direction.

Hannibal brushed her leg getting to the outside and stood gazing in the direction of the thicker trees. After a moment, the dog ambled into the yard, sniffing around the pile of stacked wood, and stood watching as several tiny wood sparrows flittered around in the bushes at the edge of the clearing. Blunt muzzle lifted into the air a moment, she turned to come back to where Samantha stood, gazing sadly up at her.

"Don't ask me, Hannibal," she said. "I just work here. I have no idea how long we'll be here nor what we're going to do with that master of yours. I need follow-up instructions, believe me."

With one last look at the unfriendly clouds overhead, she stood aside as Hannibal took her time going into the kitchen, measuring the distance to a warm place by the stove before collapsing in her selected place.

Checking to see that Nicholas appeared to be sleeping, Samantha added more water to the pot on the stove and went to complete the unsavory task of washing the breakfast dishes.

It was almost noon on a Monday morning, a Monday morning she was supposed to be off-duty, relaxing and finishing her Christmas shopping. Instead of roughing it in outdoor camping she normally enjoyed, she was semiroughing it with an irritated giant who caused strange misbehavings to her insides.

"Must be my age," she mused aloud. "Perhaps Mums is right and I should get married and start a family before I get too old. But, as Emily so thoughtfully inquired, where will I find somebody big enough for me?" One came to mind, but he was already taken with a tall, willowy beauty back in civilization.

There was no point in dwelling on that thought, so she went to find her book.

The story didn't hold her interest, and she put it down to check on Nicholas. He was still asleep so Samantha put another log on the fire, stirring the coals until the flames licked energetically around it.

The shaggy head that covered the pillow and his beard would be the envy of a beautician who tried unsuccessfully to strip hair the way his was mixed, dark and light blond. No artificial coloring would lend such uniformity as was evident there. Nicholas said he didn't have a comb, but she had a wide-toothed lift in her handbag that would serve much better than a regular comb.

In the kitchen she picked up her handbag and rummaged through zippered pockets until she pulled out the hair lift so popular with the current kinky hairdos. Her hair was far from kinky, but the tool lifted the deep waves of her thick sandy hair to make it look as though she had just left the beauty salon.

After pouring hot water over the wide plastic teeth of the comb, she dried it by waving it in the air and walked back toward the bedroom. Hannibal rose to follow her and stood watching doubtfully as Samantha paused before her master, looking down into the peaceful face.

She really shouldn't wake him, but... "Nicholas," she said softly and smiled as he turned glazed eyes toward her. "I found something that I can use on your hair and your beard. Maybe it'll make you feel better."

He mumbled something she didn't think was complimentary, but she proceeded to comb and straighten his hair, her long fingers smoothing it along the teeth of the lift and untangling it. He didn't protest, so she continued with her task until he looked neatly brushed and combed. She stared down at him, satisfied with the performance and wanting badly to run her fingers through the now-smooth hair.

Startled at the intense feelings, Samantha took a step backward, looking down into wide-open blue eyes. "What time is it?" he asked, his voice sounding loud in the quiet room.

Swallowing hard, she glanced at her watch. "Two o'clock on Monday afternoon," she told him.

He frowned and she forgot her feelings as concern for her patient took over. "Do you feel all right?" she asked.

He moved his good arm restlessly, reaching across his body to rub the injured shoulder. "No, I'm not all right," he said shortly.

"I'll massage you," she told him. "That will relax the tension a little."

"No." He turned away and closed his eyes again. "Don't bother."

Almost wanting to shake him, she opened her mouth to let him know how she felt about big boys feeling sorry for themselves when it was they who had done the damage, when she heard the unmistakable sound of a car door slamming outside. Nicholas heard it, too, and turned to look at her with questioning blue eyes.

With a sigh of immense relief, she said, "I hope that's your Dr. Knight. I could use a good sounding board right now, not to mention some help with a difficult patient."

Hurrying from the room with Hannibal at her heels, Samantha opened the front door and looked outside to see not Dr. Knight's truck, but a white Lincoln Continental Mark V.

A feeling of dread consumed her as she stepped outside to see Dr. Knight emerge from the passenger's side of the car, walk around to the driver's side, and open the door to allow a tall, slim beauty to alight. With the elegance of royalty the beauty queen glided toward her, and Samantha stiffened at the glance of dismissal the lovely girl allowed her.

Dr. Knight extended his hand, smiling. "Miss Bridges, it's so good to see you again. Tell me, how have you been?"

She nodded and the doctor continued with his speech. "This is Valerie Brewer. Mr. Jordan's fiancée."

Chapter Five

Silently Samantha stood aside as the two people entered the cabin; she was glad she had spent a few minutes earlier sweeping dust and trash from the wood floor. As Valerie Brewer passed, a wave of expensive perfume enveloped Samantha and she almost sneezed. Her eyes went over the slim figure in a red pantsuit that shouted Dior, dark hair lying on her shoulders.

Closing the door, she waited for Dr. Knight to speak. "Tell me, Miss Bridges, have you had any trouble?" His look was anxious.

"Not really, although Mr. Jordan's quite restless today. His fever went down and he's eating better."

"May we ...?"

The question was interrupted by the bull-like bellow from the next room. "Sam!"

She smiled. "He's awake."

Valerie moved quickly ahead of them to the closed door, disappearing inside the room, but her voice was plain. "Oh, Nick, darling, I've been so worried." The voice became muffled, and Samantha bit her tongue picturing the reconciliation that was taking place out of her sight.

Dr. Knight smiled apologetically. "Miss Brewer has been very concerned." Samantha nodded and he went on. "I brought more medical supplies and groceries, but let's hope he can be moved in a few more days. What's your opinion?"

"The sooner you move him, Dr. Knight, the better. He's so big I've not been too successful in turning him."

"I tried to find someone to come to stay with you, but there's a shortage of qualified people all around. Mr. Jordan's father is in Copenhagen and will be home next week, but until then I'm afraid you'll be alone again." He walked toward the bedroom, his glance taking in the pot on the stove with boiling water, the neat array of glasses on the counter.

He knocked lightly on the door and went in when a muffled voice answered. Samantha remained where she was and was still staring at the door when Dr. Knight opened it and beckoned her.

She stepped inside the room, her glance going immediately to Nicholas. Valerie sat on the edge of the bed, holding his uninjured hand on her lap, smoothing his neatly combed hair from his face. Rather than bright, the blue eyes that stared at her were dim. Samantha frowned and moved to the head of the bunk, close enough for her fingers to touch his forehead. He was much warmer than he had been a few hours earlier.

"You must move him, Dr. Knight. No one can stay in this primitive place as sick as he is," Valerie said and murmured to Nicholas who closed his eyes. "Heaven knows how they'll get all this hair off and shave him. He looks like a caveman."

Samantha's eyes went to the face Valerie described, and she nodded in agreement. He did resemble one of the oversized cavemen pictured in history books, and she could imagine him with a club in his hands dragging his girl friend behind him after successfully capturing the one he chose.

She loved his beard, but somehow she couldn't picture Valerie Brewer in the role of captured girl friend being dragged to his rock castle.

Dr. Knight approached the bed, and Valerie reluctantly moved away as Samantha moved closer. "Let me do a little checking up on you, Mr. Jordan," he said.

Nicholas opened his eyes and looked at the doctor, then turned the direct gaze toward Samantha. "Sam's taken good care of me, even if she is bossy."

A ghost of a smile touched Dr. Knight's face as he met Samantha's eyes and turned to the patient. "I'm sure she has, Mr. Jordan," he agreed and began his examination.

Samantha ignored Valerie, although she was conscious of the woman's restless prowling around the room, standing near her sleeping bag a few moments then moving to the fireplace, occasionally tapping her expensively shod foot.

As Dr. Knight straightened, Nicholas asked, "Well?"

The doctor nodded. "You're doing much better, Mr. Jordan, but I'll have to wait until the weekend to move you. A helicopter will come in Friday. The company has arranged for one to be specially outfitted for you so there's no danger of reinjuring any of those smashed bones, and by then you should be able to stand the trip into Los Angeles.''

"Los Angeles?"

Samantha, too, turned questioning eyes to the doctor. ''Yes. They have a special team of orthopedic surgeons standing by to operate on you as soon as we can get you there.''

"And my chances of walking on this leg again?" Nicholas asked, his voice tight.

"Fifty-fifty."

Valerie came swiftly to push Samantha aside. "Oh, Nick, you poor darling." She bent and kissed him on the mouth, and Samantha stiffened, turning to take Dr. Knight's stethoscope and repack it in his bag.

She set the bag aside and turned to add another log to the low fire as a means of occupying her hands, hands that would rather have wrapped themselves around the lovely throat of the woman crooning over Nicholas.

Pity he didn't need. She didn't want to admit it wasn't the pity that angered her but the fact the girl's mouth had touched the firm lips she wanted to kiss herself. Mentally she gave herself a vigorous shake and went to the kitchen, aware that Dr. Knight followed close behind her.

As she entered the room, Samantha found Hannibal standing near the closed bedroom door and sympathetically she pushed it open enough that the dog could join her master.

A moment later Valerie said, "Oh, Hannibal, you smell like a dog. You can't stay in here." Evidently the low voice that spoke said the dog could stay because she didn't reappear, and Samantha knew a moment's satisfaction that Valerie didn't get her way with Hannibal.

"Miss Bridges, I know this is hard on you, but as Nicholas said, you're doing a fine job. Weather allowing, the helicopter will pick him up on Friday."

Dr. Knight went through his bag. "Here's a different drug for the pain shots. As he gets stronger, he may move too much and he'll suffer for it. Just don't let him try to sit up, and keep adjusting the harness lower for thirty minutes at a time, then back up to the height it is now."

"He looks as though his fever has gone back up, although it was normal this morning."

He nodded. "It's almost one hundred, but this is not unusual in cases such as his." He frowned, taking his glasses off to wipe them. "Let's hope he doesn't get any kind of viral infection from having to lie flat so long."

"I'll watch him," she said. "Would you help me change the bed sheets before you leave?"

They went back into the bedroom, eliciting a dark look from Valerie when she had to move away from Nicholas while they struggled to get clean linens on the bed. They were both sweating and breathing hard as they finished, but Samantha knew it would be much easier on Nicholas not to have wrinkles beneath him.

As they turned to leave once more, Samantha felt the daggers from Valerie's dark gaze.

"I'll get those groceries from the car," Dr. Knight said, and she followed him outside. The damp breeze smelled like rain, and Dr. Knight gave a worried look at the low clouds but made no comment.

Together they carried four bags of groceries inside and left them on the table. "I'll put them away." She began unpacking them as he went toward the bedroom and knocked before entering. Samantha finished putting away the groceries, marking a couple of items for their dinner. There was even a half gallon of fresh milk.

"Oh, Dr. Knight, did you bring in the books for Nick?" Valerie asked.

"I didn't see them."

"On the back seat."

"I'll get them," Dr. Knight offered and left them.

As soon as he was out of sight, Valerie turned to face her. Samantha could read her mind before she spoke. "Well, this must be a tiresome job for a woman out here alone with a strange man." Dark eyes went over Samantha's figure in pants and a sweater, satisfied she had no competition there.

"It's quite isolated," Samantha said agreeably and, tongue in cheek, added, "but being alone with a strange man doesn't bother me." Let her make of that what she would.

Dr. Knight's entrance halted what the other woman would have said. He placed a hardcover book and a thick magazine on the table while looking at Samantha and smiling a little.

"You'll have to hold it for him as it's quite heavy, but it might interest him during the wait for the helicopter." He drew in his breath. "I'd feel better if there was a phone somewhere nearby, Miss Bridges, but maybe the bad weather will hold off until we get you both out of here."

"Bad weather?" she asked. "Is there a report out on something?"

"Yes, a storm system is moving in from the coast, and they expect heavy rains in this area. Fortunately the cabin is far enough from the river that flooding won't be a problem."

"I certainly hope not. I can swim but I believe Mr. Jordan would find it difficult." The old familiar anger at the situation came through in her voice.

Dr. Knight heard it and nodded, picking up his bag. He held out his hand to her and said, "We all appreciate the fine job you're doing, Miss Bridges."

Samantha followed them to the door and watched them leave, feeling only relief even as she looked at the stormy sky overhead. As the car disappeared down the trail, she turned back into the cabin, busying herself with the fire in the stove before she went into the bedroom, taking the thermometer with her.

Dr. Knight had adjusted the harness holding the injured leg, and she looked to see how far he had moved it before she looked at Nicholas. He was watching her, eyes half closed.

She touched his forehead. "How do you feel, other than terrible?"

Dark lashes settled against his cheek. "Don't be facetious."

"Miss Brewer is beautiful as described. You should feel much better." She tried to keep the envy out of her voice, not sure if she succeeded. "She looks beautiful as well as rich."

His lashes swung upward to reveal his bright eyes, but he didn't answer her, closing his eyes again.

His wrist felt warm to her fingers as she counted his pulse. Slipping the thermometer into his mouth, she waited, her glance taking in the figure of the giant on the bed. Dr. Knight had dressed his shoulder, changing every bandage he could, and it had tired her patient.

Her concern deepened as she read his fever at one hundred and one degrees with a fast pulse.

"Damn!" she said quietly, reaching for the lotion by the bed, beginning her massage on the good hand, working upward to his shoulder. He flinched as she moved across his chest.

"Where did I hit a tender spot?" she asked.

"To the left of my neck about two inches."

"I didn't touch there," she told him.

His voice was tired. "It felt like you did."

Samantha went on with her massaging, careful to keep her fingers light as she moved over all his exposed skin.

She went to get the hypodermic needle, reading the directions on the new bottle before filling it and returning to the bedside.

"This will hurt, Nicholas," she told him. He didn't answer nor move as she gave the shot and covered him again, remaining beside him, thoughtful gaze taking in the trussed-up, still figure.

Why did she feel he and Valerie Brewer weren't the same type? A man as handsome as Nicholas could surely have his pick of women, in or out of his social strata.

Not only was Valerie Brewer thin and beautiful, but if the car was any indication, she was also not in the working class of people. So what did it matter if Nicholas Jordan was a logger? Who said he couldn't meet a rich woman and fall in love with her the same as a poor one? Such a logical thought stayed on the surface of her mind and didn't penetrate any further. She resented Valerie Brewer.

Turning away, she faced Hannibal, sad, pointed eyes looking from her to her master. Samantha stooped and held out her hand, and the dog took one step forward and laid her heavy head in the outstretched hand. Samantha's long fingers smoothed through the thick wrinkles, brushing the silky hairs that stuck out like inch-long bristles from the layers.

"I hope the women who got coats from those skins get fleas, Hannibal," she said. "I don't know how it can be, but as ugly as you are, you're cute and cuddly somehow." She smiled into the anything-but-alert eyes. "Just like Nicholas: big and beautiful."

She rose from her kneeling position and went toward the kitchen, Hannibal a step behind her. It was six o'clock and time for dinner.

A quick check of both fires showed them to be doing well, and she scouted the items she had selected from the new groceries. A while later, she arranged an attractive plate of chicken and dumplings, iced tea, and pear halves for Nicholas.

His head was turned away from her, but as she stopped near the bed, the heavy lashes moved on his cheek and he swallowed.

"Nicholas?" Placing the items she carried on the table, Samantha touched his forehead; it was too warm. She frowned, moving quickly back to the kitchen to take the thermometer from the mug she used to sterilize it. She went back to pick up the hand lying on his stomach. Ignoring the little pleasurable sting that went up her arm, she was all professionalism as she concentrated on his pulse, watching the thermometer stuck between his lips. The figures she recorded on the chart caused an uneasy chill to settle in her stomach as she met the dull blue gaze now turned her way.

"Did you tell Dr. Knight that you were feeling worse than earlier this morning?"

He sounded tired. "I told him I felt rotten, but he seems to think that's normal." His body jerked. "What do you know about the orthopedic team in Los Angeles."

"Nothing. If I had any say about it, I'd make sure you went to Alistare in Chicago. The best bone surgeon in the world operates there." She smoothed his pillow. "He costs a mint, but if your company's insurance covers it, that's the place for you."

"Write down the doctor's name and that hospital address for me and put it with my clothes."

"What clothes? What wasn't torn off you had to be cut to pieces to get you out of them." She picked up the plate and fork. "Besides, how do you propose to get pants on over that?" She nodded toward the contraption that held him immobile.

"I hadn't thought about it." He opened his mouth as she put food near it and swallowed with what she thought was difficulty.

Suddenly he grinned up at her. "You mean all that's between you and me are these bedclothes?"

Darn her fair skin, anyway, she fumed, as she felt the color come into her cheeks. You'd think a twenty-nine-year-old woman could do something about blushing every time a particular man makes smart remarks. She couldn't remember the last time she blushed before meeting Nicholas.

"Behave, Nicholas, and eat your dinner."

"I'm not hungry, and my throat hurts."

Samantha groaned inwardly but held the glass of tea up for him. He sipped only a little before shaking his head. Without another word, she took the plate and glass with her to the kitchen, rounded up pills and syringe, and returned to the bed. Hannibal sank in a heap near her feet.

"I'll get to you, Hannibal. Just give me a few minutes." Soaking cotton in alcohol, she turned the sheet back without looking at Nicholas, gave him the shot, and turned to hand him the glass to swallow two tiny yellow pills.

"What are they?" he asked.

"You wouldn't know even if I told you, Nicholas. Swallow them. That's the only way they work—inside you."

She could see the effort it took to get the pills down his throat but said nothing more. Her fingers were cool against the warmth of the big neck as she felt under the beard on his chin for the glands that were wide and swollen. She pressed gently and he glared at her.

"Do you take Vitamin C?" she asked.

He snorted as much as he could manage with his sore throat. "I'm never sick. Why should I take medicine?"

"Just because you're a big, strong outdoorsman, doesn't mean you get enough vitamins in all your food.

Besides, Vitamin C is not medicine, and everyone needs it whether they're sick or not. When you get back to civilization, I suggest you start taking them—after you've seen a doctor, of course."

"I guess nurses can't resist telling everyone how to take care of themselves," he said, trying to make his voice nasty, but failing because of its huskiness, which only made it sound sexy...as if he needed any help there.

"You're right, but think about it and you'll decide that it won't hurt a thing to help out nature a little bit."

His eyes went over her big frame as she stood smiling down at him. "My body feels like it's dry enough to crack open. Massage me."

Samantha let the little-boy demand in his voice go over her head. "Let me take these things back to the kitchen before I start that. Are you sure that's all you can eat?"

"Yes."

"Back in a minute," she told him and went into the kitchen. She fixed Hannibal's food, and washed her hands before she returned to the bedroom, detouring slightly to put a log on the fire.

His eyes were closed as she began the gentle but firm rubbing of the medicated lotion into his skin. It was firm muscle and skin beneath her long fingers, and she gave herself over to concentrating on the benefit the massaging would be to Nicholas rather than the pleasure it gave her to touch him.

His uninjured leg moved beneath her stroking fingers and she looked up to meet his gaze. Neither spoke and as he closed his eyes, she let her breath out slowly, until then unaware she had been holding it. A brief moment later she went on with her task, going across to the exposed foot of the broken leg. His left hand was the last part of him to rub, and she filled her hand with lotion to work between his fingers, over his palm and down his wrist. An inch behind the wrist bone was a wide pale circle she assumed had been left by a watch.

As she finished rubbing him, she leaned to put the bottle on the table, and her hand was captured by his free one that had been lying innocently still until that moment.

"What is it, Nicholas?"

"Do all your male patients fall in love with you?"

"Of course, especially all of them in isolated cabins who have no one else to fall in love with."

He made an impatient move with his head. "Are all the nurses at your hospital like you?"

"Do you mean bossy?"

He squeezed her fingers lightly. "Yes, I guess that's what I meant." He released her hand and turned his head away.

Samantha stood watching him for a moment, covered him with the blanket, and went into the kitchen to see that Hannibal had disposed of her dinner and was waiting patiently by the back door to be let outside. It was dark, but she could hear the wind and feel the dampness as she waited for Hannibal to amble back into the room and drop near the stove.

The books Dr. Knight had brought in were on the table and she stopped to look at them. One was a heavy trade publication on lumber and building materials and the financing of the same. The hardcover book was

Sidney Sheldon's latest bestseller. She went to look for her paperback mystery.

Her concentration on the story had been broken so many times she couldn't get interested in it and finally put it down to go check on Nicholas, uneasy about the fever and sore throat.

Let him get pneumonia and this would be her last private-duty case with a fat paycheck, she thought as she eyed him professionally. He lay quietly, but she didn't know if he was asleep and didn't want to disturb him if he was.

Pulling the sleeping bag nearer the fire, she sat on it, arms around her knees, staring dreamily into the flames. So romantic, she thought, and jumped as Hannibal pushed her unironed muzzle through the opening between her arm and her body. She scratched behind the small pointed ears, triangular like her eyes, lying almost flat against her blunt head. The dog flopped, her body running altogether like an accordion, part of her on Samantha's lap, and yawned, showing a tongue that looked as though it had small flowers painted on it.

"Lord, don't tell me you have strep throat, too," she said. She pried the jaws open to get a closer look at the oddly marked tongue.

"It's flowered," Nicholas spoke from the bed.

She turned to look at him, still holding Hannibal's muzzle. "Flowered? A dog's tongue?"

"I told you she was unusual."

Letting the dog go, Samantha got up and went to the bed. "You two certainly belong together," she said.

His eyes were still closed, but his lips parted in a slight smile. "Am I unusual?"

"Well, I haven't had many patients seven feet tall that hang off the bed on all sides," she said.

The glare wasn't quite as forceful as it had been, but it was there just the same. "I'm only six feet six inches tall."

"Close enough," she told him, her hand unobtrusively touching his forehead and going to the lumps in his throat.

"I'm thirsty."

"I'll be right back," she promised and went to get orange juice. She put ice cubes into a glass, poured the juice over them, and went back to her patient.

"I don't have any straws, but maybe you can manage. It may burn your throat a little, but swallow these aspirins with it." Samantha popped the pills in his mouth and gave him the juice. He grimaced as he swallowed and took another drink, lying back on the pillow with a groan.

"It burns like fire."

"I know," she sympathized, "but they'll help." Looking down at him, she asked, "Dr. Knight said your father's in Copenhagen. What's he doing over there?"

"Combined vacation and business trip that I was supposed to be on. I knew I shouldn't have been such a conscientious son, staying home to let him go. Then I wouldn't have been here when the fire started."

"Who talked you into staying here?"

He opened his eyes only an instant. "Valerie."

Naturally, she thought, fixed his covers, and asked, "Will he be there for the operation?"

"Both my parents will be, knowing them." He smiled a little and turned toward her. "So will Noelle."

Noelle. The delicately feminine name brought to mind another beautiful, petite woman, and Samantha gave an inward groan at the thought of another gorgeous girl friend waiting in the wings.

"And who's Noelle?" she asked, not really caring to hear the answer.

His eyes went slowly over her face, all the way down the front of the well-filled beige sweater. "My sister," he said. "She's just as pretty as you are."

I'll bet, she thought, picturing his kid sister with bright blue eyes and worshiping her big brother. But at least, it was a sister, not a rich, lovely female competing for his favors.

He moved restlessly, and she bent over him. "Would you like to try eating again?" she asked.

"No." His good leg came from beneath the covers, and she pushed it back, pulling the blanket over it again. "God, I hurt," he said.

"I know." She smoothed his hair back, relieved to find his forehead much cooler.

"What's today?"

"Monday."

He lay still without talking any more, and a moment later was breathing easily. The shot, combined with the pills and aspirin, had finally reached him and he slept.

In the kitchen she restoked the fire and got ready for bed, following Hannibal to the sleeping bag near the fire. She stretched out and relaxed, turning her back to the dog who shared her sleeping quarters.

A moment later, the beast came around to her side, slithered to the floor, and lay with her squared nose a few inches from Samantha's face. They stared at each other a moment in the dim firelight, closed their eyes, and went to sleep.

Chapter Six

A thundering crash, followed by a startled yelp and Hannibal's frantic headlong dash to share her sleeping bag, jolted Samantha awake. Half asleep, she wrestled with the dog's quivering body pressed against hers as she sought protection from the noise.

"Heavens," she muttered. "How can something as ugly as you be afraid of a mild thunderstorm?"

As if to convince her of its seriousness, bright lightning lit the room followed by another roll of thunder that bounded between the mountains, shaking the small cabin, the rumbling still echoing as Samantha struggled from the sleeping bag.

"Come here, Hannibal," a quiet voice spoke from the bunk. "At least I appreciate real beauty."

She looked toward Nicholas, checking automatically to see that he was covered and still on the bunk, then back at Hannibal, who cowered at her feet.

"Go on," she encouraged the dog. "He's big enough to protect us all."

Ignoring both of them, she put wood on the fire and stirred the hot coals to flames before putting her robe on and going to the bed. Hannibal huddled near Nicholas, accepting his big hand as a sedative to calm her nerves.

"How are you this fine morning?" she asked, her fingers on his pulse, one hand touching his face, lingering for a moment on the thick bearded cheek as she checked the glands. Her face warmed at the smothering feeling in her chest as she straightened his covers, checking the harness, and looked back at him.

His eyes were wide open, clear of the feverish film that had been evident yesterday. "I think I could run the Boston marathon today," he said.

"A little wet for that, but we can train indoors," she told him. She glanced at her watch, which showed six-thirty, Tuesday morning, October thirteenth. Good thing it wasn't Friday, she thought, her superstition showing. Anyway, it was going to be a long, long day for Nicholas Jordan if he was beginning to feel well enough to be sarcastic.

Confident he was a lot better, she went into the kitchen and, for once, Hannibal wasn't under her feet as she put wood in the stove and more water on to heat. She took the bedpan to Nicholas, ignoring his dark look as she left it with him.

At the back door she looked out on a dark, unfriendly, definitely wet, morning. Rain slanted in near-solid streaks, splashing in the puddles already forming on the saturated ground. Lightning played over the treetops and thunder rolled like a drumbeat toward Yakima.

"I hope Dr. Knight's right about the rivers being too far away to bother us," she said aloud and went to the pantry where she had seen a jar of Tang and some honey.

Dog and master lay with eyes closed as she reentered the room, and she placed the breakfast plate on the table by them. Hannibal's wrinkles lifted, but it wasn't worth the effort for her and she let them drop over her eyes again as Samantha bent over Nicholas. Removing the bedpan, she returned with a washcloth and shot paraphernalia and wiped his face and hands before taking capsules from her pocket.

Well aware of his unwavering stare, she held the glass out to him as she put the capsules in his mouth and waited for him to swallow.

"I'll give you your breakfast before it gets cold and the shot afterward."

"If you'll put the plate on my chest, I'll feed myself."

"Fine. Call me when you want a drink."

As he ate, she dragged the sleeping bag to the corner of the room and went back to the kitchen to fix her breakfast, taking her plate back to sit near the bunk and eating from the small table.

Sensing his eyes on her, she turned to smile at him and took his fork as she gave him the glass of Tang she had mixed with milk and honey.

"Whatever it is, it's good," he said.

She nodded. "Dr. Knight brought fresh milk, and it makes a good drink.

"Are you a health nut?"

"Not to the extreme, but I don't go much for carbonated drinks and fast foods." She looked down at her full figure in sweater and pants. "I just eat too often and too well."

She met his smiling blue gaze and wondered if her accelerated heartbeat showed through the knit fabric as he surveyed her generously proportioned body. Completing his survey, he lay back on the pillow and closed his eyes without comment.

"Didn't they even leave us a radio?" he asked after a short silence.

"No, but I have one in the van I can listen to if we think it will help us any. We can't go anywhere no matter what happens, but I'm sure Dr. Knight will keep an eye out for emergency conditions up here."

He turned to look at her then. "Does the company pay you well for duty like this?"

"So I've been told." She smiled. "Why?"

"You're on twenty-four-hour duty. If you belong to a good union, you could get a good bit of cash for a deal like this."

"Yes, I could. However, in the interest of your well-being, I'll forgo riches to get you back to civilization and the proper care for that leg."

He grinned. "Spoken like a dedicated nurse." His blue gaze slid down her front, then back up to her face. "You really don't have to explain being alone with a stranger to your boyfriends?"

"It's not difficult to explain to doctors. They know how these things go, and someone has to do it."

"Do you date many doctors?"

"Not many."

"Many nondoctors?"

Really, Nicholas, she wanted to say. *Have I asked you how many Miss Brewers you date?*

"I manage to fill my social calendar to my satisfaction, Nicholas. I must admit that sometimes my social activities give way to unplanned duties. Such as the case I'm on now."

"What kinds of duties do you prefer, Sam?"

"Healthy people," she replied promptly.

He tapped her wrist with one long forefinger. "You wouldn't have a job if we didn't have a streak of misfortune once in a while."

She sighed. "I never have to worry, Nicholas. I can always depend on the likes of you. And Benjy."

"Who's Benjy?"

Her voice softened as she thought of the small boy she had cared for so many months. It would be a long time before he was strong enough for the marrow transplant they were investigating as a possible benefit before he went through such a painful ordeal.

"Benjy's our five-year-old semipermanent resident at the hospital where I work. He has soft bones that keep him from walking much, but not from getting around. He can cover more territory crawling on all fours than I can with my long legs."

"He's crippled, too?" His lips disappeared into a straight line as he frowned at her.

"Not 'crippled, too,' Nicholas. He'll never be able to walk as well as you do. After you're operated on, no one will ever know you were hurt unless you show them the scars. But, Benjy...." She shook her head. "Benjy's chances of ever walking normally are one in a million. Or less."

In the silence that followed, Samantha could see Nicholas digesting that bit of information, could almost see the wheels of thought turning behind the darkened gaze that went over her again.

"When you see someone small like that and you're helpless to do anything for them, how do you cope with it?"

"By hoping research will come up with a cure, by watching the medical experiments to see anything that looks hopeful." She smiled down at him, at the serious questioning of his expression. "We also check out any genies we meet, in case one might have a magic lamp."

"I always thought nurses and doctors were indifferent to their patients, that they couldn't afford to become too involved or it would make them ineffective."

A sudden surge of anger stiffened her. "Look, Nicholas, I don't know what your association with the medical profession has been, but the staff at Young Memorial is anything but indifferent. Of course, we don't cry over our patients—at least, not where they can see us. However we do let them know we have sympathy for them. Regardless of what you've heard, we are human."

"Why, Sam, you have a temper," he teased. "I thought I'd never get anything but a calm, reassuring response out of you." He chuckled and a shot of adrenaline slid along her veins. It had the same effect as if he'd touched her. He sighed, a tired sound, and she realized they had talked a long time.

She picked up his plate and turned to go. "Sam," he said. "If I had to do such a stupid thing as get hurt, I'm glad they didn't find that male nurse."

Looking over her shoulder at him, she saw his eyes

were closed but a tiny smile curved his mouth. She wanted badly to return and touch that smile.

Swallowing, she went out with the dishes and returned with the shot she knew he needed to make him more comfortable. As she raised the sheet, his eyes opened wide to watch her. Disconcerted, she averted her face so he couldn't see her expression as she deftly administered the shot, swabbed the spot with alcohol, and covered him again.

In the quiet of the room, the drum of the rain was plain, but the growling of the thunder had retreated over the mountains. Hannibal remained as close to the bed as she could get, sighing occasionally.

Leaving the two of them, Samantha went to do her chores, getting everything ready for the next go-around of medicine and shots. She let Nicholas sleep, and when he stirred and moaned, she went to give him his bath.

"I'll do it," he said as she wet the cloth. She handed it to him and put a bottle of lotion by the fire to warm. When he finished his bath, she took the lukewarm lotion and began smoothing it on his face, rubbing the liquid on his forehead, over his cheek and nose where the skin had peeled.

His lips were dry and she touched a few drops to them, her fingers no longer rubbing but caressing because that's what they required of her. The tip of his tongue came out to touch her fingers, and her eyes flew up to meet the directness of his.

"I like that," he said quietly.

I love it, she wanted to say, continuing her massage down his uninjured arm, pressing hard on the big hand

and long fingers to improve circulation. Without speaking, she squeezed more lotion in her hands, working it into his heavy thigh below the towel covering him, kneading the muscles, circling his kneecap with firm pressure from the heel of her hand.

When she finished with his right leg, she examined the pulley holding the broken one, letting it down as Dr. Knight instructed her to do, and flexed the big foot before she started rubbing lotion into it.

"If you were ticklish, we'd have a problem," she said, applying a generous amount of lotion. He didn't answer and she went on, "You know, of course, once you're in orthopedics this foot will also be in a cast."

"Why?"

"When they operate, they'll want this side of you to be absolutely still so the bones heal right, and to do that, you'll need to be in a cast from your hip down."

He didn't say anything for a moment, then asked, "What about the shoulder?"

"It isn't broken, only dislocated. Aside from soreness, once it's manipulated completely back into the socket, you'll have a single sling to support the arm and won't have it bound as tightly as it is now."

"I should be thankful for that?"

"Yes, you should." She completed the massaging and stood up. "If you saw the holes where the tractor decided to play cowboy, you'd wonder how you got out with a few broken bones." She turned away.

"Sam."

Glancing around at him, she waited, but his eyes were closed and she walked back to the bed. "Are you all right?"

"Yes. I wanted to tell you that you paint such pretty pictures with your hands." His eyes opened and he gave her a mischievous grin. "You don't have much of a canvas to practice on, but I have a great imagination."

Uncontrollable fiery color flooded her face. "You're incorrigible, Nicholas." This time she left him without a backward look.

The rain continued all day long, and Samantha set about heating water to pour into the bottom of the fiberglass shower stall to soak the bedclothes Dr. Knight had helped her remove. It took several heatings in the biggest pan she had before there was enough to cover them and, when she finished that, she looked around to see how she could dry them. The small table and two spindly legged chairs would have to be used for the job.

A peek into the bedroom showed Nicholas with eyes closed and Hannibal still within his reach. She smiled at the picture and went to look for her book she had put down so many times.

The books Valerie had brought Nicholas lay on the table, and she picked up the one by Sidney Sheldon, letting the stiff new pages flip until her finger blocked them. Skipping down the page a few lines, she read a paragraph describing a love scene. Samantha continued reading until the words blazed on the page. She swallowed hard and felt warm color come into her cheeks at the vivid description that left no detail to the imagination.

"Sidney doesn't paint pretty pictures; he splashes them in living color," she murmured as she replaced the book on the table and opened the magazine. It was mostly advertisements for lumber materials and by-products, and she looked at pictures of beautiful homes built from the advertised goods.

All the money spent on one of those homes would build an entire subdivision in suburban Yakima, but they were nice, she admitted to herself, giving them one last look before she closed the cover and picked up her mystery.

At lunch Nicholas was untalkative, giving the appearance of wanting to sleep more than anything else, so she left him alone.

Hannibal decided she had to go outside, even if it was still raining, but was back in record time.

"Don't blame you at all," Samantha told her. "In addition to being beautiful, you're also smart." Hannibal gave her a disdainful look and went back to lie by the bed. Nicholas's right hand dropped to her back, rubbing behind the box-shaped head.

In the small shower room she struggled with the sheets, sloshing them up and down and wringing them. Her hands were strong, but she was out of breath when she decided she had enough water out of them to hang them across the table and chairs arranged near the stove.

"Makes me appreciate my ancestors who didn't have Maytag appliances," she said as she finished the chore and opened the refrigerator to see what might be interesting for their evening meal.

"Sam!"

"The master calls," she said, hurrying toward the bedroom to stand over him. "Yes, Nicholas?"

She'd never get used to that direct blue gaze that seemed to find new things about her to explore each time she was near him. Several seconds passed before he gave his request.

"Valerie said she brought some books. What kind?"

"A lumber mill advertising journal and Sidney Sheldon's latest bestseller."

"Can I see them?"

"You can look at the colored pictures in the magazine but, really, Nicholas, I think you're too young for Sheldon's masterpiece."

"Have you read it?"

"Only the pages that had holes burned in them," she said.

He grinned. "That good? Maybe you should read that one to me."

"Not on your life, Nicholas. My mother would wash my mouth out with soap, not to mention tan my britches."

"Does your mother know you're staying with me? Alone?"

She laughed. "No, Nicholas, and please don't tell her. She thinks nurses lead very dull lives on the three-till-eleven shift every night with no time off. Don't disillusion her."

His eyes fixed curiously on her. "Really? She doesn't know you're on a private-duty case way out in the middle of nowhere with a stranger? An eligible bachelor." He smiled. "Very eligible."

"That's right."

"Why?"

"First of all, she wouldn't understand. Second, she doesn't care to hear the details of my very uneventful life. Third..." She shrugged. "And so on."

"Are there any more members to your family?"

"Just the one sister I mentioned."

"Is she a nurse?"

"No, she works for the utility company in San Antonio." Adjusting the harness a little, she smoothed the covers, touching his forehead with light fingers, and turned to get the books for him.

Taking a small glass of the Tang mixture back with her, she handed him two aspirins. The ease with which they were swallowed indicated the glands were almost normal.

"What's the date on the magazine?" he asked.

"October first," she said, after checking the front cover.

He nodded and reached for it, managing it deftly in the big left hand, turning pages with his right.

Leaving him with the magazine, she went to start their meal. Because of the dark clouds and rain, the single light bulb had burned all day and, as night came, it seemed to give off very little light. Her glance went over the stack of wood by the wall. She would need to bring in some more to dry before all of that was burned.

Dampness penetrated her clothing before she was outside. She shivered but ran to gather an armload of wood to place near the stove. In those few minutes she was wet and forced to change clothing. Her gown had gone into the wash and was still damp around the seams, so she took out the uniform she had packed and put it on.

The sameness of the food is beginning to be humdrum, to say the least, she thought, as she fixed a plate to take in to Nicholas. Hannibal raised her head and sniffed, and Nicholas put down the magazine to see what was on the plate.

"I'm hungry," he said.

"That's a very good sign. When you start complaining about what you get to eat, you're completely cured."

"As long as you're my cook, waitress, and nurse, I won't complain, Sam."

He continued to look at her as she cut the meat and moved his pillow a bit higher. "You look different in the uniform. What happened to turn you into the professional-looking Miss Bridges?"

She grinned. "I got wet bringing in wood and smelled like Hannibal."

His look darkened. "I'll bet you've had very few jobs where you had to rough it quite this rough."

"It's not bad, Nicholas. Look at it this way. Out here I have only one bedpan to empty, one patient to look after, one..." She looked down at the dog. "Sorry, Hannibal. Not that you don't count, but you do sort of look out for yourself, except in thunderstorms."

"Most dogs are afraid of thunder. It hurts their ears," Nicholas defended Hannibal.

She nodded. "I know lots of people scared to death of thunderstorms." Emily, for one. Samantha felt a fierce satisfaction, remembering her sister's intense dislike of storms, a time she wasn't the beautiful, self-assured business woman, lording it over her big sister.

Handing him a fork, she said, "Eat before it gets cold." With a swift once-over to see that everything was within his reach, she said, "Come on, Hannibal, and I'll fix your personal banquet."

As Hannibal gobbled up her dinner, Samantha sat relaxed at the table, eating slowly, letting her thoughts wander back to her daily routine at Young Memorial, wondering about Benjy.

What had Leo done over the weekend if he didn't catch duty again? Would Myers Reston forget she was due to have this coming weekend plus Monday and Tuesday off because of the postponement for this pet project of his?

He'd better remember; I'll be the first to remind him if he even looks as if he wants to forget about it. When it came to her time off from the job she loved, she became fierce about it, believing that people in the medical profession needed relief from daily association with illness and death, resenting comments about nurses having it made when they looked forward to their long weekends off between shifts. She sighed, thinking of the grueling hours worked before the time off came along.

"Sam!" Nicholas was definitely better. The bellow was getting to the demanding stage, a prelude to requests to get up or, in his case, getting up without a by-your-leave.

"Yes, Nicholas?" She took the plate from his stomach, brushed a crumb from the sheet, and handed him the glass. "Did you get enough to eat?"

He nodded, drinking the liquid and handing the glass back to her. "I'm tired." He grimaced. "How can I lie here and do nothing and be this tired?"

"It's worse than working, they tell me," she said.

"Aren't you ever sick?"

"I've been very lucky, health-wise."

"You think luck is the answer?" he asked, watching her curiously.

"Luck in the way that I didn't inherit any bad health from my ancestors. And I do try to take care of myself." She didn't mention her obvious weight problem.

She went on to take care of the ever-present cleanup duties and came back to him with a warmed bottle of lotion. Ignoring the blue eyes fastened on her as she began the massage, Samantha concentrated on the firm skin she rubbed the lotion into, paying particular attention to his hands. When she came to the injured arm, she pried his long fingers apart, checking for swelling, and breathed an inward sigh of relief when she found none. His shoulder was doing fine.

Her fair hair swung down as she bent over to press her fingers into his hard thighs, working her way quickly down to the knees, then squeezing the muscles in the calves of his leg, and continuing on down to the fine anklebones. His right foot showed no signs of swelling from nonuse, but she pummeled the sole to stimulate circulation. His left foot showed some light blue discoloration near the end of the homemade splint, and she worked several minutes on the exposed area.

"Is that sore?"

"Yes."

"Well, why didn't you say so?" She looked up, frowning.

His eyes were closed. "I was enjoying it."

"Enjoying pain?"

He grinned without opening his eyes. "Your touch makes pain exquisite, Sam."

For no reason she blushed, feeling the warmth passing through her hands, which were still holding his foot, and through her body. Carefully she put the foot back on the pillow where it had rested and adjusted the covers around him.

"A shot will help you rest better as well as sleep," she said. "I'll be right back."

"Sam." She stopped and waited for him to go on.

"You do more for me than any shot or pill." He turned his head to smile at her. "I recommend your bedside manner to all sick people."

"Your company pays well for my bedside manner, Nicholas," she told him and went out, staying in the kitchen long enough to let the trembling leave her legs.

Samantha had been warned of nurse-patient love affairs, but this was ridiculous, she fumed to herself. The man did terrible things to her blood pressure, and he didn't know she existed aside from her hands painting pretty pictures when she massaged his tired body. He'd go back to his job and lovely fiancée and never remember his nurse who got all excited over his giant-sized thighs.

Shaking herself mentally, she went back to give Nicholas a shot. For a moment she was tempted to jab him unnecessarily to get his attention, but the nurse in her forced her to gentleness as she took care of the job at hand. She handed him water and two capsules and went to put a log on the fire.

She looked at the dog. "Come on, Hannibal. The rain's stopped, and you need to see how dark it is outside."

Studiously avoiding his blue eyes, Samantha gave

Nicholas one last check and left him. Her paperback mystery lay on the table, and she picked it up while she waited for the dog to return.

It wasn't long—one short demanding bark and Samantha opened the door to let her in. Hannibal, more than slightly damp around the edges, stood quietly as Samantha took one of the towels she had washed by hand and dried the bristly hair.

She smiled into the pointed eyes. "You know, Nicholas may be right. Perhaps you are beautiful. You just take some getting used to." She rubbed the towel over the stub of a tail and patted her almost with affection. "Just like your master."

Chapter Seven

Nicholas was still asleep as Samantha made her way quietly into the kitchen to dress and let Hannibal out into the drizzly morning. Although her watch said seven o'clock, it was dark outside and she could see only Hannibal's shadowy outline as she sniffed a few times and came back into the house.

Samantha turned to the ever-present duties to attend to in a sickroom and went back to see if her patient was awake. His eyes were closed and his big hand lay relaxed by his side. Her trained eyes took in the firm mouth, molded perfectly beneath the heavy beard, lips slightly moist, his breath deep and even. If there was any fever at all, it was slight and she blessed their luck.

Luck had a way of running out, she thought, but she'd better not borrow any trouble by guessing what could happen without warning.

Her gaze went from the shaggy head on the rumpled pillow to the leg held in traction. The blanket had slid away, exposing a broad expanse of golden-brown hair on his chest, his waist, and belly. As big as he was, there was no fat, only firm skin stretched over hard muscle. Whatever job he had in the lumber camps or mills, he could handle from sheer brute strength, she was sure. Looking at the big hand held motionless by the bandages, she thought that if he should ever take a notion to hold her to keep her from doing anything, she would be the helpless one.

Let's hope you remain a gentle giant, she thought. She smiled as she pulled the blanket back to cover him, touching his face as she did so. It was almost cool.

"Hello, Nicholas," she said as he opened his eyes.

With a scrutinizing look, his gaze traveled from her neatly brushed short hair, over her straight nose, and lingered on her soft mouth innocent of lipstick, showing small white teeth as she smiled. His eyes went down to the green-checked flannel shirt she wore, opened enough at the throat to show the lift above her full breasts.

"You're nice to wake up to in the mornings, Sam," he said finally without smiling. "Are you always so cheerful?"

"Yes. It takes my unhappy patients to make me grumpy. Cheer up, Nicholas. It could have been much worse."

"It also could have been a lot better if not for careless. . ."

She spread her fingers over his lips, feeling his warm breath on them, and with an effort forced herself not to withdraw them quickly as the thrill whispered its way through her body.

Hoping he couldn't read her feelings, she said, "I know, but we can handle it."

"I like the way you're so free with this 'we' stuff. I'm

the one who'll be crippled the rest of my life. 'We' have nothing to do with it.''

"Think positive without feeling sorry for yourself, Nicholas. Before you give up, get an expert diagnosis from people who know how to take care of injuries such as yours."

He made an uncomplimentary sound and turned away from her, and after a moment she went for the hated bedpan and left him looking sourly after her.

Bath, shots, and pills later, she fixed their breakfast and sat near him as they ate, looking at him only to check if he needed any help.

He was managing fine, but the dark look remained on his face. Samantha sympathized but was darned if she'd let him know how she felt. Anyway, if he had any idea what just looking at him did to her heartbeat, he'd have a field day with her. Her emotions had never before given her any trouble around patients unless it was her sympathy for them, but she admitted to having a problem with Nicholas Jordan. She frowned at her almost empty plate.

"What's wrong? Indigestion?" he asked, his voice taunting her.

Straightening in the small chair and glancing at him, she said, "You could say that."

Her conclusions were hard to digest, that was for sure. There was no way in the world that five days with a cantankerous patient could result in her falling in love with him. A very eligible bachelor, he said, with a beautiful, possessive fiancée.

Quietly she got up and gathered his dishes, handing him the glass to drink from before she went into the kitchen to heat more water and clean up a bit. Startled at what she had admitted to herself, she kept busy as long as she could, then was forced to stand by the small window to gaze at the ugly weather outside.

Hannibal brushed against her leg, and she glanced down at the dog who looked appealingly back at her. Kneeling, she put both hands behind the small ears that flattened against an undistinguishable forehead that ran without interruption from nose to thick neck. The golden eyes regarded her unblinking, until Samantha laid her cheek against the five-o'clock shadowed muzzle. After a moment a rough tongue caressed her face and a wide paw lay on her shoulder.

She stood up. "All right. You've won my undying affection but only because you belong to Nicholas," she told the dog. "Let's venture into the weather and see if my car will start. I may have to make a run for it, and I don't want to let the battery die. Maybe we can pick up a weather report, for all the good it'll do us."

Taking the red jacket from a nail behind the door, she stepped to the bedroom to look at Nicholas, who lay with eyes closed, but she didn't speak to him.

Outside, she stood with Hannibal, looking around the denseness that enclosed them in a very small world, breathing deeply of the wet air. The burned smell was still with them.

"Come on, Hannibal, you can get in with me. The seats will wipe clean." She opened the door, and without hesitation Hannibal climbed into the van to sniff at the new-smelling upholstery, giving her approval as she sat down.

"I'm glad you like it," Samantha said, putting the

key in and turning it, smiling when the motor purred to
life without hesitation. Dependability—just what she
needed, she thought, satisfied more than ever with the
van.

Switching the radio on, she twirled the knob across
the dial. All she got was growling static, testifying to the
fact that they were, indeed, closed in and away from
everyone, including weather forecasters. With a sigh
she turned the radio off, muttering to herself and
glancing at Hannibal who rested contentedly beside
her.

The dog was in no hurry to leave the dry inside of the
van, but Samantha opened the door on her side and
said, "Come on. It's warmer in the house."

They walked around to the back, and she gathered an
armful of wet wood to take inside and place near the
stove to dry out. Friday was still a long time away if the
rain continued, and right now it showed no signs of
letting up.

"Sam!"

No wonder he never calls me Samantha, she thought
on the run. *As many times as he calls me, he has to
shorten it.* Hannibal raced her to the bedside of her
master, rearing on her hind legs to place a paw on his
arm and lick his face. He patted the dog, looking past
her to Samantha.

"I thought you were leaving me," he said.

"Why would I leave such a nice, sweet person all
alone up here in the wilderness?" she asked, eyebrows
raised, her long fingers resting on his wrist, counting
automatically. His pulse was steady, something she
couldn't say for her own.

His grin was sheepish. "Do I give you a rough time?"

Using her best judgment, she dénied it. "Of course not. You're a model patient."

"That doesn't say much for the models you use."

"I don't have anything to say about which ones I get. They're foisted off on me at a moment's notice, playing havoc with any plans I might make." Not to mention other things that get splintered when one runs into an unexpected force, she added mentally.

Checking the apparatus over him and the shoulder bandage, Samantha went on, "The van hadn't been started since Saturday, and I didn't want the battery to die down in case we might have to use it for an emergency."

"What kind of an emergency are you expecting?"

"You don't expect emergencies, Nicholas. They're just there when you least need them. You of all people should realize that." She tugged at the harness, letting it down two inches. "I tried to get a weather report on the radio in the van, but all I got was static. We're socked in as the meteorologists would say."

He made no reply but his wince was audible. She turned to look at him to see his lips were pressed together. "Does that hurt when I move it just that much?"

"Yes." A thin film of perspiration appeared on his forehead.

Uneasy, she pulled the harness back to its original height and went to get the pills and lotion. He took the capsules without a word and closed his eyes as she began massaging his legs.

The several minutes it took to complete her ministrations to him were silent minutes in which she sought to keep her unprofessional thoughts in line, succeeding only a little. Friday had better come on time—and, even so, she could still get into deep trouble before it arrived.

With an impatient shrug of her shoulders, she went into the kitchen to fix lunch, taking her time to get her feelings under control before she faced Nicholas again.

She put a piece of the dry wood in the stove and added a wet piece that would burn more slowly but keep warmth in the room. The cabin was well built and small enough to heat without much trouble. Even so, she felt a draft and looked out the small window on the back wall to see the trees bending in the wind. How she wished the radio had been a little more responsive.

She wanted to know what was about to happen before it did, but what would she do about it if she did? Shrugging, Samantha finished their sandwiches, put soup into bowls, and uttered a sigh for the girl who, after all these years of enjoying male companionship without commitments, found herself with deeper-than-normal feelings for an almost-total stranger.

Her patient watched as she prepared to serve the light meal to him and handed him a spoon for the soup.

"Did I ever mention that I dislike soup of any kind?" he said. The quiet question caught her by surprise. She had expected some curt remark about her failure to get a weather report over the van radio.

"No, never," she said.

He took a spoonful of the tomato soup to which she

had added some of the powdered milk and a generous square of margarine. Continuing to eat, he looked back at her when it was all gone.

"I didn't want to make you unhappy by being finicky about eating."

"What do you like to eat, Nicholas?"

"Oh, oysters Rockefeller, lobster, What-A-Burgers."

Her nose wrinkled. "Oysters are blah."

"Did you know you have freckles?" he asked, studying her face.

"Left over from summer."

He picked up the sandwich made from canned corned beef and bit into it. "Where did you go on vacation this past summer?"

"The week of the fourth of July, we camped out up near Chinook Pass and did some hiking."

"You and your sister?"

She laughed. "Not likely. Emily doesn't leave air-conditioning and hot baths for anyone."

They ate in silence for a moment, Samantha aware of his glance coming her way between bites, but she gave her attention to slipping a piece of her sandwich to Hannibal.

Nicholas broke the silence. "Whom did you camp with?"

"Dr. Jarvis, one of my favorite medical doctors."

"Male?"

She looked up at him. "Yes, Nicholas."

She didn't offer him an explanation, wondering if he would believe that she and Leo shared a lot of time together without getting closer than brother and sister.

Few people would, but she had never before cared what anyone thought and frowned because she wanted to make it clear to Nicholas.

"May I have a drink?" he asked. She handed him the glass from the table.

They finished eating in silence, and she removed the dishes and cleaned the small area in the kitchen, checking both fires and adding wood. Opening the back door to look outside, she shivered as the cold wet air hit her. The temperature had dropped several degrees since she and Hannibal had been out, and the trees swayed in the stiff wind.

Taking capsules with her, Samantha went back into the bedroom. Nicholas stared at the ceiling, his right fist opening and closing as it lay on his chest. His gaze riveted on her as she stood by the bed, but she didn't speak as she offered him the medicine and the water, helping him lift his shoulders and head in order to drink.

"Would you like to read?" she asked.

He closed his eyes. "No. You read to me."

She placed the glass on the table. "All right, but somehow I really don't think this book is the right one for reading aloud. It's more for hiding under the covers to read after lights-out time."

"Who's your favorite author?" he asked.

"James Joyce." She didn't look at him as she opened the book to the foreword and went on to page one.

He chuckled deep in his throat, and she caught her breath at the sound, looking back at his face. His grin was wide, showing big white teeth beneath his heavy beard, blue eyes narrowed and bright with laughter.

My Lord, he's handsome, Samantha thought and stiffened. She hadn't thought about what he looked like other than being bigger than life, but he was definitely attractive. She bit into her lip as she realized anew the danger she faced.

Never before had she been afraid of a patient, not even the ones who were physically hard to handle, but she was afraid of Nicholas Jordan. Afraid of his physical touch and afraid of her own emotional response.

Two more days, she counted. *Heaven help me act as a nurse is supposed to act until I can get him out of here.*

"If you read Joyce, a few of Sheldon's graphic descriptions shouldn't bother you. If I remember correctly, his books were banned for years until they were reluctantly printed."

"He was a literary genius," she said.

"And not a little pornographic."

"Do you want me to read to you?" she asked as the deep sound continued in his throat.

His right hand came out and touched her cheek. She jumped, pulling back as his fingers lingered only a moment before dropping to her shoulder to slide down her arm, catching the hand that held the book open. His hand literally swallowed hers, and although her fingers were long and slender, they disappeared within his as he rubbed his thumb over her knuckles back to her wrist.

"Lovely hands," he murmured and released it to put his hand back across his chest, closing his eyes again.

Taking a deep breath, Samantha began reading, feeling easier as the first part of the novel went into a description of the city where the first scene was to take place. Several pages later, she hadn't run into any of the scenic artistry that made her apprehensive about reading aloud to Nicholas.

He appeared to be asleep, and she sat quietly watching him, her eyes again those of the professional nurse, looking for signs of swelling, for signs of discomfort other than the tiredness he complained about.

Don't let anything happen to keep that helicopter out of here, she prayed to whoever might be listening. *We're pushing our luck, leaving him like this without expert attention to those bones.*

She stood up and placed the book on the table and turned, almost stumbling over Hannibal, who gave her an indignant look and moved exactly one inch.

Both fires needed attention and Samantha was busy for a while, checking food for their evening meal, bringing in wood to place piece by piece near the stove and fireplace so it would dry. The wind was cold and wet as it whistled around the corner of the cabin. Hannibal wasn't interested in going out into the mess, and she didn't blame her.

Her own book lay on the table, and she opened it again but managed to stare at two pages before she put it back and walked to the window to stare out into the early twilight. There were no solutions to the problems outside, so she gathered capsules and aspirins, put them on the counter, and went to check on Nicholas.

The room was in semidarkness, but the fire made it seem cozy. She stirred it, placing one of the damp logs on the one burning brightly. Turning toward the bed, she saw her patient's eyes were open, staring at the ceiling. She had seen the set look before, one of depression and a what's-the-use attitude.

The lotion bottle was by the bed, and she took it to pour some into her hands to massage him, beginning with the big hand lying on his chest, working it into his fingers. He didn't move as she continued to rub, even as she touched his thigh where he usually gave her at least one teasing glance. Worry began as he lay still, allowing her to continue without any comment.

"Nicholas?"

"What?" His voice was hard and tight, his body straight and tense.

"Don't give up on me, Nicholas," she said, her voice placating. "I know you're in pain and I know you're worried, but the surgeons they have waiting for you know how to treat this type of injury. You have a better-than-average chance of being as good as new."

He glared. "What's average?"

"I mean..."

"Why would you choose the surgeon in Chicago over the ones in Los Angeles then, if they're so good?" he demanded.

"I know the ones in Chicago; I don't know who's in Los Angeles."

"Did you write down the doctor's name in Chicago?"

"But, Nicholas, arrangements have already been made for you in Los Angeles, and they're standing by to take care of you as soon as you arrive. You don't just have a team of doctors waiting for you and not show up on a whim."

"It's my body they'll be cutting on and my legs that I may not ever be able to use again. I think I should have a say, don't you?"

"It isn't my decision, Nicholas. I have nothing to do with it."

"I do. Write down the doctor's name you mentioned." He turned his head away, dismissing her, and she stood a moment looking down at him, tempted to pull his shaggy head against her and cuddle him.

As she went to look for a pen to write down the name he wanted, she almost smiled. Imagine cuddling something as big as Nicholas. Better she should tangle with one of the wild black bears running loose in the Cascade Mountains. She found a pen and slip of paper in her handbag and wrote down the name of the orthopedic surgeon who headed the world's most famous team of bone specialists. She had had the good fortune of being in the operating room with him as he worked on a prominent movie star injured in a skiing accident. For a moment, she wondered about the insurance company and decided they'd better be willing to let Nicholas have his way or they might have more injuries with which to contend.

Gathering capsules and syringe, she went back to the bed, knowing just how he must feel. The past several days had been nothing but rounds of the same thing— shots, pills, bedpans, bland meals, and start all over again with the same aching, tired body.

Hannibal hadn't moved, nor had Nicholas. Placing the items on the table, she reached for his hand, fingers moving over the smooth skin of the inner wrist. As her thumb rested on the wiry hairs on the back of his hand,

Samantha felt familiar electricity pass through her, reflecting the awesome masculinity in just a touch of her patient.

He turned his head to watch as she counted, and she placed the thermometer between his lips, smiling at him as she did so. He lay still as she gave him the shot and took the glass of water from her without a word, but his eyes continued to go over her face, down her body, and back again.

Warmth flooded her, but she bit her tongue and finished taking care of him, noting with relief that his temperature was only ninety-nine degrees. With a body as big as his, that could be his normal temperature, but at least it wasn't dangerous.

Bent over to gather the articles to return to the kitchen for the next go-around, Samantha was unprepared for his sudden move. The unrestrained right arm came around her, pulling her to the bed. His left hand caught her arm, holding her without effort as he slid his hand up her back to pull her against his chest.

"You smell like a baby," he murmured. "And you're so soft."

Hands planted against his chest, she pushed, but she might as well have pushed at a thousand-pound boulder. Lying awkwardly on top of him, she opened her mouth to yell at him, but his hand pressed her into him, moving up behind her neck to bring her mouth to his.

His eyes were so close, she could see the tiny veins in the corners. Aware as she had been of the electricity, she had never seen blue the exact color of his eyes. The blond-brown beard was rough on her cheek, but the sensuality of its touch wasn't lost on her as her parted lips were closed by the force of meeting his.

The world spun as he held her, his mouth moving on hers, finally ceasing its wanderings to increase the pressure, gently questioning the feel of hers, finally letting up enough that the tip of his tongue caressed lightly across her mouth.

The fingers of his left hand moved upward over her breast, back and forth, leaving her feelings flaring from nerve centers inside her that she never knew existed. It was as though he touched her in many places at once—her thighs, her lips—drawing a red-hot line across her stomach and back to the breast he caressed with slow, deliberate movements.

"Sam," he murmured.

"Let go, Nicholas."

"No, Sam, it feels good to hold you. Stay close to me." He didn't give her a chance to do otherwise as the big hand on her neck spread, holding tightly as he sought and found her mouth once more.

Her breath came from deep within her chest as she tried to get away from him. She didn't have to worry about hurting him; he was holding her so that she could only protest. There was no way she could maneuver to get her arms free nor to release her body from contact with his.

"Stop fighting me, Sam," he whispered against her lips. "I like the way you taste, and I want you to taste me."

His lips took a caressing path across her cheek to the

pulse tripping beneath her ear, but before she could take advantage of catching her breath to tell him to release her, he claimed her mouth once more.

This time the kiss was different. He demanded her response, spreading flames from his hands down to her feet, and for an instant she pictured the forest fire licking uncontrollably through dry trees and underbrush, erupting into all-consuming heat just the way her entire being was doing for Nicholas.

His hand moved downward across and under her hips, lifting them to bring her all the way against him. It was her chance to free her lips but she didn't, instead exploring his mouth, tasting the warmth inside, accepting the sudden thrust of his tongue, giving herself up to feelings Nicholas was awakening. Both hands moved upward to frame his face, letting him keep her body as close as he needed her to be, answering his desire with her own.

Her fingers slid over the roughness of his beard, down the thick neck, over his bare shoulder, digging into heavy muscle on his arm as he tightened his hold on her, bringing his hand up under her sweater, releasing her bra. The heaviness of her breasts, free of their restraint, thrust against him, and he bit gently into her lips, his breath coming quickly, as she was held to the broad expanse of his chest.

The fingers of his left hand were unrelenting as he held her; the other hand worked around her shoulders, under her arm to close over her breast, stroking the fullness, his thumb making circles over the rosy tip that grew rigid at his touch.

A log in the fireplace broke, sending crackling flames

higher, lighting the dimness of the room for an instant, and she lifted her head to stare into his face.

He was breathing heavily, eyes closed as he continued to hold onto her.

"Don't, Sam," he whispered. "Don't leave me."

A thin film of perspiration lay on his forehead, and she could feel his chest move with his rapid breathing. Slowly realization came that she must be hurting him even though he showed no signs of releasing her.

"Nicholas," she said, her voice barely audible, "let me go."

His hold on her tightened, if that were possible, but she stiffened away from him, bracing against his uninjured arm to push her body upward.

He opened his eyes. "Will you come back?"

"Yes, Nicholas," she told him, standing on her feet as he suddenly opened his hands, freeing her. Her legs threatened to buckle as she leaned against the bunk, looking down at him, her thoughts anything but those of a professional nurse.

She moved away to busy herself with the fire, biting her lips to stop their trembling, the sensation of the print of Nicholas's mouth still on them. Without looking at the bed, she went into the kitchen and stood at the small dusty window, staring into the deepening dusk without seeing the trees bending or the black clouds settling over the dense forest.

Forcing herself to move, she went outside to bring in several armfuls of wood. As she turned, she found Hannibal yawning in the doorway.

"You'd better get your business finished and get back inside, lady," she told her. "I think we're in for another shower or two." She watched heavy clouds sailing across the sky and turned, finding it necessary to watch where she was going as complete darkness fell.

Automatically she went about getting their dinner, trying to use her imagination to make the meal attractive. There was enough of everything to make a Spanish omelet, but she was tired of cheese and eggs, and Nicholas probably was, too. So far, he hadn't complained about any of the food she served except the soup—and he even ate that. When he complained about their menus, he'd be on the way to recovery.

Recovery—and removal from her keeping where she would be safe from his reaching arms. But not safe from the power he had over her to bring all her feelings she never knew she possessed to clamor for fulfillment.

The pulse in her throat hammered, threatening to cut off her breath as she thought of their passionate encounter. Passionate wrestling match. She was no match for Nicholas whether he was half crippled or not. He was without a doubt the strongest patient she had ever had, and she might have to hurt him to force him to keep his hands to himself.

But she knew she would never hurt Nicholas—not if she had anything to say about it.

Hannibal sauntered into the kitchen, shaking water from her bristly coat, and Samantha turned to close the door behind her. Rain was falling in sheets, blowing sideways in the stiff breeze.

She opened a can of food for Hannibal and heaped it into the dish, which was emptied of the meat with one swift slurp. Leaving her crunching on the bits, she took Nicholas his plate.

He watched her walk toward him, taking in the well-filled sweater, the bra obviously refastened. As she put the plate on his chest and handed him a fork, he asked, "Aren't you going to eat with me?"

"I'm not hungry."

"Then sit with me," he said.

Samantha shook her head. "I'll be back with your medicine when you finish eating," she told him, turning away.

"Sam."

"Yes, Nicholas?"

"Look at me," he ordered.

Turning back toward the bed, she stood four feet away from him, well out of reach of his long arms. "What do you need, Nicholas?"

He grinned. "Literally?"

He was so much like Benjy when she couldn't make up her mind whether he needed a spanking or a hugging. She made her voice severe as she said, "You're talking about what you want, not what you need. Fortunately I know the difference, whether you do or not."

His eyes went over her. "Tell me the difference between need and want, Sam." He smiled and put the fork on the plate. "Come here and tell me."

Melting inside at the look on his face, she turned away. "Call me when you finish eating."

In the kitchen she stood looking at the plate she fixed for herself, finally putting the contents in Hannibal's dish and watching her dispose of them without any problem.

"You go ahead and get fatter. You'll soon be out of my life, and you and your master can eat your oysters Rockefeller and lobster. Be overweight; see if I care."

She sat at the small table, chin in her hands, staring

reflectively at the chair at the other end, her thoughts on the man in the next room. He had started fires inside her that up until this time she had only read about; the fierce desire described in stories taken from the vivid imaginations of writers was alive within her, taking over where common sense had deserted her.

Nicholas Jordan was her patient, left in her care until he could be moved, and she couldn't afford to fall in love with him. She had seen patients fall in love with their nurses, but it was a natural reaction when patients thought they couldn't survive without the care given them. The love usually lasted until the patient was returned to the outside world and found he could manage again without the nurse's attention.

How many times she had seen the phrase "uncontrollable desire" written in books, extolled in love songs, thrown carelessly around by people impressed by circumstances? But it had never applied to her—until now. She had an uncontrollable desire to lie close to Nicholas, to let their bodies explore each other.

But Nicholas would be leaving her two days hence; he would return to his world of cutting logs and Valerie, perhaps not exactly in that order.

"Poor Nick." Aloud she mimicked Valerie's pitying voice. "Poor Nick, my foot," she said to Hannibal as she got up from the chair. "That's like pitying King Kong."

Samantha fixed the shot and capsules and went into the bedroom. Nicholas had finished eating—the plate still resting on his chest—and was staring at the ceiling with the look that made her uneasy.

"Would you like a glass of milk? You may as well drink it while it's still fresh."

His stare was disconcerting as it went over her from the top of her sandy-blond head to the white nurses' oxfords she wore, finally coming back to meet her eyes.

"All right," he said.

When she came back with the milk, he was half sitting up, his right arm stiffened to support him. "No, Nicholas," she said, hurrying to reach him. "You'll hurt yourself that way. Lie back down."

He allowed her to ease him back on the pillow, but he was holding onto her as she tried to back away from the bed. "Go with me when I leave here Friday, Sam. I won't mind the operation if I know you're there with me."

"You know I can't do that. The team of surgeons will have their favorite nurses to use for such delicate jobs."

He pulled her down so that she was forced to sit on the side of the bunk. "If I arrange for you to go, will you?"

"What would Valerie think of such an arrangement?"

He smiled. "You're my nurse, a valid reason for being with me. Besides, Valerie won't have to know you're going."

"Don't practice your deceit with me, Nicholas Jordan."

"What's deceitful about wanting your favorite and trusted nurse to accompany you in a life-and-death situation?" he asked. He caught both her hands in the big right one, pulling her to him.

"Life and death for whom? The doctors if they hurt

you?" Without haste, she extracted herself from his hold and reached for the milk.

"It's an operation they've performed successfully hundreds of times. You're a big boy and can stand the pain that will go with it. When it's over, you can brag to your buddies how brave you were to go through with it after saving all the timber for the forest animals and the lumber companies."

He lay back breathing hard. "I don't have any buddies."

"You have Valerie," she said.

He closed his eyes. "Yes."

She wanted to hold his huge head to her breast, wanted to smooth the shaggy hair and run her fingers through the thick crispness of the waves. Her fingers closed tightly around the glass she was holding.

"How about Noelle and your parents?"

He opened his eyes then, and after looking straight up at her for a moment, he grinned. "You're right; it'll be good to see them."

She handed the glass to him with a capsule. "How long has it been?"

"They've been gone six weeks, but it seems longer."

"Must be nice to travel in Europe that long on vacation," she said, taking the glass from him as he obediently swallowed the capsule.

He didn't answer immediately, and she put the glass on the table, turning once more to check the fires. "Sam?"

Continuing on with what she was doing, she said over her shoulder, "Yes, Nicholas?"

"Will you go with me for the operation?"

"No." She wasn't sure if it would be possible for her to go, whether the company he worked for would pay extended private-duty fees at the rate they were paying now, but what she did know was that she couldn't go because she wanted to so badly.

"Give me one good reason," he insisted.

"Your insurance company."

"What does an insurance company have to do with whether I get my choice of nurses?"

"They're paying for me, I would imagine. Somebody is unless you want to part with a year's salary."

He stared at her. "You're that expensive?"

She grinned at him. "You bet. Good service comes with a high price tag these days." She gave him a shot and straightened the sheet and blanket, staying well out of the reach of his sudden moves. "Don't you think I'm worth it?"

"Every penny." He breathed a tired sigh. "Change your mind and go with me, anyway. We'll either convince the insurance company or find a way to pay for you."

Shaking her head without answering, Samantha went back into the kitchen to look for her book, listening to the wind and rain drumming on the roof and beating against the windows. Stoking the fire in the stove and adjusting the damper, she got ready for bed and sat holding the book for a while, her mind on the man nearby.

When she returned to the bedroom, she saw his face was turned away from her, and she pulled the sleeping bag nearer the fireplace, crawling into the space, smiling at Hannibal who wandered over, dropping in her now-reserved spot nearby.

Sleep eluded Samantha, and against her better judgment, her thoughts went to Nicholas: the way it felt to be held in his arms, the warm sensuousness of his demanding mouth on hers, wrapping her in a scarlet mantle of desire.

It was far from her first kiss, but it wiped out the memory of all others. With a sigh at her foolishness for falling in love with an untouchable patient, she finally slept.

A feeling of uneasiness woke her and Samantha turned to look toward the bunk before she moved from the sleeping bag. Only a glow remained of the coals in the fireplace, and her hand outside the covers was cold. Shivering as she wrapped her robe around her, she moved quickly to put a log on and stir the coals until a tiny flame caught.

Nicholas didn't move, and she went into the kitchen, stirring the coals to life in the stove and adding wood. She was putting water on for coffee when Hannibal strolled into the room, stretching her wrinkles a little as she yawned, her pointed eyes only half opened. Standing in the middle of the room, Samantha listened for the wind and rain, but there was nothing, really a peculiar sensation to her ears. She started toward the back door when she was startled by a loud cracking noise from the outside.

Hannibal's eyes opened as wide as possible, and the small ears pointed sharply forward as she, too, stared at the door. They both moved at once, and Samantha was conscious of the low growl coming from the dog's throat. It sounded vicious; she had never so much as barked or made any noise other than the occasional loud sighs.

Samantha slid the lock back and turned the knob only to find the door stuck. Yanking with her considerable strength, she pulled it inward and stared at the fairy-tale world outside. During the night the temperature had dropped sharply, and moisture on the trees and bushes had frozen solid, leaving a sparkling crust of ice on everything. The sound they heard was the breaking of a tree limb not strong enough to hold the weight of frozen water.

Hannibal sauntered past her to stand on the small porch, gazing at the sight that confronted them. Samantha closed the door behind her and she, too, stood silently looking around them.

"Just what we need, Hannibal," she said. "However, I'd have appreciated it more around Christmas."

The dog put her square nose to the ground and walked gingerly into the yard, sliding precariously as she tried to keep her footing. She looked around at Samantha for reassurance and found none.

"Sorry, lady, I can't help at all," she answered the imploring look directed at her and went back into the house. Uncertainly she shook her head and went to check on Nicholas.

He was still asleep; the noise from the cracking ice had not disturbed him. Without touching him, she put her hand near enough to his face to feel that his temperature was normal, and she breathed a sigh of relief. As she turned away, a big hand closed over her wrist and she looked into blue eyes that were wide awake.

"Good morning, Sam," he said quietly.

"Hello, Nicholas." She didn't try to pull her arm away but used her free hand to find the pulse in his left wrist. It was strong and steady.

"We have a small problem today," she told him.

Holding onto her hand, he gazed silently up at her, searching her face aglow in the firelight. He tugged at her arm, pulling her down to sit beside him.

The smile was lazy, separating firm lips beneath the beard, showing remarkably white teeth. "If the problem's small, the two of us should be able to solve it with no trouble."

She shook her head. "Not that small," she said. "Unless the weather changes for the better, the helicopter won't be able to come in here tomorrow."

"Why not?"

She tried to withdraw her hand, but he held on, and she knew it was useless to struggle. She explained about the ice.

"The temperature must have taken a sharp drop suddenly, and everything's frozen solid. Hannibal is very put out."

He frowned. "What will it mean if the trip's postponed a couple of days?"

"You need that operation now, Nicholas; the sooner the better. We don't want your bones to start knitting together in the wrong position. We'd be in big trouble."

His hand tightened. "How big?"

"If that should happen, the bones would have to be broken again and reset. It is *not* fun."

He looked down at the hand he held and moved his

thumb across her knuckles to the inside of her palm, letting the thumb slide across the soft inside of her hand. A strange feeling of heat followed his gentle caress like a magnet, and she pulled away from him to stand up out of his reach. A sharp command at the back door indicated Hannibal was ready to come inside, and she used that as an excuse to hurry away from him and open the back door for the dog. Hannibal gave her an accusing look, shook the moisture from her wrinkles, and trotted toward the bedroom. Samantha heard Nicholas extend his sympathy and stood a moment, leaning against the door to rearrange her thought processes before she went about performing the routine morning duties.

With a pan of water and washcloth, Samantha approached the bed where Nicholas lay staring at the ceiling. He must know every crack and cobweb in the area visible to him, and she felt her heart go out to him. An outdoorsman chained to a bed must find it impossible to deal with the fact that he had many, many days coming to be spent in the same way, staring at a ceiling in this room, a hospital room, and his own room where he would be convalescing for an even longer time.

She dipped the cloth into the warm water and squeezed the excess from it. Nicholas took it in his right hand and wiped his face and both hands. Giving it back to her, he rubbed his neck and chin. "I must look like the original hairy ape."

She laughed and he turned his head to look directly up at her. "You could use a few shaves, I guess. You mean you don't usually wear a beard?"

"No." He continued to look at her. "You have a

lovely laugh, Sam." He put his forefinger on her arm. "You're lovely all over."

Her brows lifted. "All over?"

He grinned, closing his eyes again, and amended his statement. "Well, almost all over."

"I'll be back," she promised without getting into the "almost" part of her anatomy he had seen.

Adjusting the pillows behind him, Samantha lifted the heavy shoulders to help him sit up a little straighter without putting pressure on the bad leg. She put his breakfast plate on his chest and handed the fork to him.

He didn't start eating immediately. "Are you worried, Sam?"

She didn't try to avoid the question. "Yes, Nicholas."

He stirred the food on his plate. "Are you always so honest?"

"Would you want me to tell you I'm not worried when anyone with any common sense would be worried sick?"

She leaned toward him and this time she was the one who touched him. "Nicholas," she said and stopped. He turned the full force of his blue gaze directly on her, and her heart stopped, taking a long second before it began an irregular hammering of warm blood through her body again.

Quickly she moved her hand and sat back away from the bed, looking at her own plate. "I'm sure everyone's aware that time is not on our side, and the quicker they get you to Los Angeles, the better."

He didn't say any more, and they continued eating until he pushed his plate away. Without a word she gathered the dishes and went into the kitchen. She stared into the small sink at the dirty dishes before pouring hot water over them and leaving them to soak while she went to give Nicholas his medicine.

As she readied the syringe for his shot, Samantha was conscious of his quiet gaze concentrated on her face. Lifting the corner of the blanket she rubbed alcohol on his hip, deftly administered the shot, and covered him again. She held out a capsule and two aspirins to him.

"I don't have fever now," he said.

"I know, but they'll keep your unused muscles from feeling so tired."

He took them with the water she offered, and he patted the bed. "Sit with me for a minute."

Obediently she sat on the edge of the bed he indicated. He picked up her left hand. "You aren't married?"

She raised her eyebrows. "Don't you remember asking about my boyfriends?"

He smiled a little. "Lots of people are divorced." He rubbed her third finger. "The doctor you date—are you serious about him?"

"We're good friends, that's all." She smiled. "It happens, you know. You can truly be friends with the opposite sex without being romantically involved."

He studied her face. "How old are you?"

"Why, Nicholas, how personal you're getting."

"I just want to know all about you, and since we don't have anything else to do, we can play twenty questions." The light in his eyes teased her.

"Well, let's see. I'm twenty-nine, five feet ten

inches tall—and don't ask my weight." She drew in her breath, expanding her generous bust considerably and blushed as his eyes followed the gentle movement. She went on. "I was born in San Antonio, went to school there, attended the University of Texas in San Antonio, and went to graduate school at Baylor."

"How did you get all the way to Washington from there?"

She saw no need to go into family tensions nor the fact that sister comparisons got under her skin enough that two thousand miles seemed just the right distance between her and a constantly complaining mother.

"Young Memorial was the logical choice for a nurse who specializes in orthopedics, and I was lucky enough to be accepted there." She looked up. "And you, Nicholas? What made you choose a profession like logging?"

He regarded her a moment before answering. "Since I've always lived in the state of Washington, trees fascinate me. It isn't much fun cutting them down, but to see what can be done with them is what interests me."

They were quiet, their eyes meeting and hers sliding away. Samantha felt the familiar warmth following the solid thumping of her heart, and she tried to withdraw her hand from his. He refused to relinquish it but pulled it to his throat to lay her fingers over the pulse beating there. The two beats merged as they stared at each other; then, suddenly, he released her.

"I need to brush my teeth, Sam," he said without any show of emotion.

In the kitchen she looked for his toothbrush and a glass, wondering at the letdown she felt. What had she expected him to do? Well, for one thing— She let the thought drop and smiled to herself.

Control. Control, Sam, she thought, and corrected that, too. Samantha. She frowned. No one had ever called her Sam, and she was sure she would have objected if anyone tried it. Nicholas didn't try—he did whatever he wanted to, helpless as he might be physically.

Taking her items to the bed, she arranged his pillow higher and tended the fire while he brushed his teeth, then took the brush and glass from him to return them to the other room.

At the small window she stared with misgivings at the crystal world outside, feeling the awesome power of ice as she watched a huge tree limb sway and split like a toothpick with a resounding crash.

"Sam!"

She hurried into the bedroom to find Nicholas propped on his elbow, trying to see out the small high window across the room from him.

"What the hell was that?" he demanded.

"The ice is too heavy for the trees, and they're snapping under the weight," she explained.

He lay back, exhausted by the small amount of movement. "Come here, Sam."

She was already close by, but she stayed just out of his reach. He continued to look at her and said, "Closer."

"Look, Nicholas—"

"No wonder you aren't married; you always argue," he said, holding out his hand to her.

"We didn't finish our twenty questions," she said,

not moving. "How old are you? Are you and Valerie planning to marry very soon?"

"No to the last question. Thirty-four."

"You act like fifteen. Stop it."

He lay back against the pillow and closed his eyes. "I'm tired. Come over here with me."

Sympathy overcame her caution, and she stepped to his bedside, her hand automatically going to his forehead and then to his wrist, counting as she did so. The pulse was strong and steady. He captured her hand and held it to his chest.

"Do you want me to massage you?" she asked, her professional self taking over. As soon as he turned his head and opened his eyes, Samantha knew it had been a mistake to ask that question.

"Yes."

He let her go and she reached for the medicated lotion. Starting with his free hand, she worked her way up to his shoulder and across the portion of his chest free of bandages, down over his ribs across his abdomen. She separated the fingers of his left hand, frowning at the discoloration of the fingers.

"Does your hand feel numb?"

"It tingles a little, but maybe it's because of you."

A quick glance at his face showed no smile to accompany the teasing, and she bit her lip. "Behave, Nicholas, this is serious. Tell me when it hurts." She pried the fingers apart and pushed the forefinger backward, then the thumb.

As pressure on the thumb increased, he said, "That hurts."

She breathed easier. If he could feel pain from there,

the circulation was still good. She concentrated on rubbing briskly, going up his arm as far as the shoulder bandage would allow. Turning her face away from him, she adjusted the towel across his upper thighs, filling her hands with lotion to rub into the hard flesh of his legs. Neither spoke as she completed the job and replaced the bottle on the table.

"Don't leave," he said. "You don't have anything to do."

"You want me to read to you?"

He shook his head. "Just stay with me."

She pulled the small chair closer to the bed and sat down, giving him her hand as he reached toward her. His thumb went up each finger separately coming back to move to the inside, caressing her palm lightly. He grew still and after a few minutes, his breathing told her he was asleep. She waited, then gently extracted her hand from his, replacing his alongside his body on the edge of the bunk.

The hours dragged as Nicholas slept off and on between periods of extreme quietness that bothered her more than his teasing and demands.

Samantha gave him a light lunch and took his chart into the kitchen to study it, keeping all her notations up-to-date. Hannibal sniffed around her feet and dropped half on them to snooze, offended when Samantha stood up to go look out the window for the tenth time.

The uneasiness wouldn't go away as she stared at the icy world outside the small, cozy cabin. Any helicopter pilot with a gnat's common sense would refuse to fly into such a situation.

But they needed to be rescued for professional as well as personal reasons, she thought. She was not sure which was more urgent. She sighed.

"Sam!"

Shrugging away her rootless thoughts, she went to see what the gentle giant wanted.

"I'm hungry." He smiled, eyes still crinkled with sleep.

"That's a good sign. I'll see what I can find that might interest you."

In the pantry she checked the shelves, packed with a various assortment of canned goods. After six days of limited menus, nothing appealed to her.

"Even What-A-Burgers will taste good after this," she told Hannibal who stood near the doorway. "Not for you, however. You'll want to go somewhere they throw away meaty bones, eh?"

Selecting two cans, one of corn, the other tomatoes, she returned to the kitchen, rooting in the shelves for the jar of cornmeal she had seen. When she took the food she prepared to Nicholas, he was in his favorite pose of staring at the ceiling.

Samantha smiled to dispel her uneasiness. "When we leave here, we're never going to want another thing out of a can." She straightened the covers, conscious of his unwavering gaze on her.

"You won't forget I owe you a steak?" he asked.

"No, I won't forget."

He ate the corn fritters and the omelet with Spanish sauce made from her limited supply of spices, drinking the milk made from the dry powder he had refused at first. He made no complaints and that bothered her.

She left him and found the book she had tried to read, finishing it quickly with half an ear listening for calls from the other room. The story she started out enjoying left much to be desired, and she grumbled to herself at the unsatisfactory ending to a story that had turned flat.

"That's life, I suppose, Hannibal," she told the sleeping animal. "We never get our act together until it's too late and our hindsight shows us what we did wrong."

She added wood to the fire, noticing the small amount left from the stacks she had brought in days before. "I can see right now my first mistake a week ago was agreeing to take this duty, and I don't know yet how I can correct it."

Samantha started toward the bedroom in answer to a demanding voice. "Think what it's going to take to bring about a happy ending to this fiasco."

Without waiting for Hannibal to unroll herself to go with her into the bedroom, she went to see what Nicholas wanted.

"I drank all the water," he said.

She took the glass and went to fill it, coming back to see Hannibal sitting near the bed, her master's big hand rubbing the squared-off muzzle. His eyes never left Samantha's face as she gave him the water, and her fingers sought his wrist as a natural reflex born from constant watch for nature's warning signals.

"If it's normal, I must be dead."

"Why?" She counted the strong, regular beat and put his hand back beside him.

"You do strange things to my heartbeat, Sam," he said smiling. "You mean I have no effect on you?"

"Of course, you do, Nicholas. I can hardly contain myself."

If the truth were but known to him, he'd be impossible to deal with, and she restrained the impulse to bend to place her mouth on his.

"In that case why fight it?" He held out his hand.

Looking down at him, she suddenly realized that if the ice melted, today would be her last day with him, and Nicholas Jordan would disappear from her life the same way he dropped into it.

And good riddance, an inner voice whispered. *You're looking for trouble with this one.*

She turned away. Valerie would take good care of him once he was given back into her keeping, and she would brook no interference from such a lowly person as a nurse who took care of her boyfriend in the Washington wilderness.

"I have a deck of cards. Want to play gin rummy?" she asked.

"If you like," he said, his voice disinterested but with no more comment about the effect he had on her. She was right; he was just one more lonely and bored patient with the usual attachment to his nurse.

An hour later he handed her the cards and said, "Six out of eight wins should entitle me to something."

"It does. You can have a glass of cold milk with your pills."

"That's not exactly what I had in mind."

Impatiently she stood up, sliding the cards back into the plastic case. "Stop it, Nicholas, or I'll tell Valerie what a philandering male you are."

"You wouldn't do that, would you, Sam?" His voice

was teasing. "Isn't it your sworn duty to take care of all your patient's needs and keep all information confidential?"

Without looking at him, she went to get his medicine and a glass of milk. He winced as he tried to raise his shoulders from the pillow to accept the glass and drink, and she leaned to help him, handing him a paper napkin to wipe his mouth. Her face was inches from his and he pulled her down, his parted lips cool from the milk, touching hers lightly. He let go and she straightened.

"Good night, Sam."

"Good night, Nicholas," she answered him, moving away to check the fire and, on impulse, went to the sleeping bag and dragged it with her into the kitchen.

"Why are you moving?" the quiet voice asked from the bed.

"I slept in here because I was afraid you'd fall while you were still semiconscious. Since you're fully awake and responsible now, I'll move and give you some privacy."

"You're afraid?"

"Of course not," she denied. "Afraid of what?"

"That's what I'd like to know."

"I'll be close enough," she said without further discussion and went into the kitchen, placing the sleeping bag several feet from the stove but near enough to give her—and Hannibal—warmth during the night.

As she spread the blankets over the bottom, she tilted her head, listening to the different sound from outside. She opened the door and smiled. It was raining, which meant the temperature had risen and the ice would be melting.

"No floods," she said to the outside darkness. "Just get us out of here; that's all I'm asking."

Nicholas appeared to be sleeping and didn't mention the separate sleeping arrangements when she went to make her last check before going to bed. As she settled into the sleeping bag, she remembered the light touch of his mouth on hers. No other kiss had stirred her as much as that brief contact had done; the roughness of the heavy beard sent sprinkles of electricity across the nerves exposed by his kiss, nerves she couldn't recall studying about in biology class. Surely there were more in her mouth than anywhere in her body, especially when Nicholas kissed her.

Hannibal snored softly nearby, and rain beat against the windows, making swishing sounds as the wind became stronger.

Wind could interfere with the helicopter, too. She buried her face into the pillow. Nature had always been her ally. What had she done to incur her wrath? Fallen in love with a patient, a strict no-no in the professional world of nursing.

She awoke to a strange sight. Thin, watery sunlight filtered through the small window to form dusty shadows on the floor near her feet. The glass panes were quiet, and holding her breath, Samantha eased out of the sleeping bag and went barefoot to the door and opened it.

The ice was gone; puddles of water stood in the clearing and tree limbs hung in soggy clumps. The cold air penetrated her gown-clad figure, and she closed the door to lean against it, smiling at Hannibal who watched her with what could be termed mild interest.

"Home free, Hannibal," she said softly. She put on her robe and went to see if Nicholas was awake.

He was. "The helicopter should be able to get to us today, and you'll be on your way to proper care," she told him.

His voice was strong now. "Did you make up your mind to go with me?"

"No, Nicholas. You'll have the best of care; the best nurses are assigned to the special operations teams."

He didn't answer and was quiet as she gave his medication and bathed and massaged him. In fact, neither spoke until she moved to the injured foot.

"I'm going to rub the bottom of your foot, Nicholas. Try not to jerk away from me."

He continued to stare at the ceiling until she finished and collected the used items to return them to the kitchen. As she held the pot to run water into it, she saw the trembling of her hands.

"That bad," she mused aloud. "I didn't think anyone would ever take Robert Redford's place in my heart."

As she swept the floor and folded the sleeping bag into its compact form to carry to the car, Samantha thought of her relationship with Leo. He had kissed her a few times, but neither had pursued the act further, content to be very close friends.

She went back to check on Nicholas, conscious of his eyes on her as she walked through the door. His hand came out to her, and she sat beside him on the narrow edge of the bed.

"Kiss me good-bye, Sam," he said.

Looking down at him, she saw Valerie Brewer's eyes

dark with suspicion as she questioned why a woman would live alone in an isolated cabin with a man she didn't know for the sole purpose of caring for him. Evidently she knew little about the life of a nurse in which one was frequently called upon to perform strange duties. None quite so strange as the special duty she was on now, she admitted to herself.

"Would Valerie object?"

"Yes," he said, meeting her gaze squarely.

"Are you planning to marry her?"

"We've been engaged twice."

"Twice?"

"Yes." He lay still a moment, then smiled. "We still aren't sure."

"Aren't sure about what?"

"That we love each other enough to put up with our peculiarities through a lifetime together."

"Perhaps you don't love each other."

He nodded. "We've discussed that."

"What conclusion did you reach?"

"None. We decided to wait and see."

"How long has this been going on?" As long as she could keep the idle conversation going, she could hold off from touching him.

His answer seemed slow in coming. "Two years, more or less."

She frowned. "Nicholas, if you love her, you shouldn't keep putting it off."

"You wouldn't?"

"Listen. If I ever get engaged, it will be a very short one. If I love someone enough to think about marrying him, then it's already time to do it."

"I like your philosophy, Sam." He drew her down, holding her arm with the bandaged hand, his right arm sliding around her waist and up her back, closing the distance between their bodies. His thumb rested in the crook of her elbow, moving back and forth across the soft flesh and keeping time with the pulse that was suddenly racing.

She shifted so that most of her weight was on the right side of his chest and lowered her face to his. For an instant his kiss was gentle, but as he explored her mouth, she felt the quickening of his breath as the big hand against her back increased the pressure, locking her to him.

His mouth was hard on hers, seeking her response, and she gave it without restraint. She moved her right hand, trying to free it from his hold, and he let it go. Her first impulse was to push away from him, but instead, her hand slid over his hip where the towel had dropped away, hesitating as the firm flesh warmed her palm.

Startled at the sudden response of her body to his bare skin, she tried to lift her head, but he whispered, "No, Sam, no," and held her.

Her mouth, opened to voice an entreaty to him, was instead the recipient of his questioning tongue, across her teeth, under her upper lip, withdrawing to move in a tantalizing path along her jawline to her ear. With tiny, swift flicks, he bathed her ear with his warm breath, and as she let her body swim in the film of sensuousness he laid over her, his mouth moved back to hers, hard and demanding.

His arms were a wonderful place to stay, but danger

signals punctuated her irregular breath like radar blipping across her chest. With a twist of her body, she dislodged his arms and stood up, taking an unsteady step backward. She pushed at her tumbled hair.

"Good-byes should be over in two seconds, Nicholas," she told him, trying to control her breathing.

"It seemed shorter than that," he said, and for a moment his eyes showed a gleam she wanted to interpret as loving. It was gone immediately, and he showed no signs of having trouble with his control. He closed his eyes, and when he spoke again it was as calmly as though they had been discussing the weather for the past ten minutes instead of sending her world up in flames.

"When do you expect the helicopter?"

"I don't know." She looked down at Nicholas, resting now, seemingly undisturbed by what had transpired between them. But she was: she felt as though she moved in a world of fantasy, an out-of-focus fairy tale that could not have a happy ending. Sloughing off these thoughts, she turned away to finish straightening the cabin so it would be in good shape once they were on their way.

At the front door she looked out at her van, water pouring from the new heavily waxed paint. It would be good to get back in it and head for Yakima and the comparative safety of the orthopedic ward at Young Memorial. Even trying to keep up with Benjy would be a welcome change of pace from trying to keep up with a wayward heart that wouldn't listen to reason.

It was nearly two o'clock when she heard the uneven sound of the helicopter motor over the treetops. The rain had stopped completely, and their wet world was broken only by the sounds of the birds singing until the flying machine quieted even those.

She watched as the helicopter settled to the ground and the blades gradually stopped turning. Emblazoned on the side of the blue-and-white aircraft was the Emergency Medical Service symbol. Radio call letters were prominently displayed. Wide side bay doors opened and a stretcher rolled down the quickly extended ramp.

Two men swung to the ground, stooping automatically under the blades, and ran toward the cabin. Another man followed at a more sedate pace behind them. It was Dr. Knight, carrying his familiar black bag.

"Sam!" She was going to miss that raucous call twenty times a day.

"Yes, Nicholas, they're here."

Two hours later Samantha closed and locked the door of the cabin. For the last time she looked at the clearing, through the stripped-down trunks of the bigger trees to the burned-out area with the strong smell of charred grass and trees clinging to the wetness.

She blessed the four-wheel-drive vehicle as she moved slowly down the road that was barely a washed-out trail after the heavy rains and breathed a sigh of relief as she turned onto Highway 410 toward Yakima.

It was Friday, October the sixteenth, a day not likely to be forgotten very soon.

Less than two hours' driving time took her to the front door of her dormitory, and she unloaded her van in the quiet of in-between-busy hours on Friday afternoon. The evening shift had already reported, and the ones relieved at three were either collapsing for the weekend or getting ready for that special date.

Before she'd decide what to do she'd check her schedule. If there was any fairness in the world, Dr. Reston wouldn't have her set up for duty until Wednesday.

Samantha had little faith that her luck would hold that well. She needed time to think about the shattering effect one Nicholas Jordan had had on her well-regulated, contented life—until now.

His good-bye was etched in her mind, charring the surrounding area like the trees she had left behind.

"Sam," he had said as they loaded his body, leg contraption and all, onto a wide stretcher preparatory to putting him on the helicopter, "if you'd go with me, I wouldn't mind the operation, just knowing you were there."

He squinted up at her in the light from the doorway. His voice was strong, but he spoke only for her ears.

Shaking her head, she smiled, trying to hide the worry she felt about the operation, wishing she could go with him, knowing she couldn't. Besides the prohibitive costs, she couldn't stand the thought of being with him through the operation only to be sent packing as soon as it was over. Better to end it now before something happened they couldn't undo.

Nicholas needed her reassurance and expertise as a trained and highly specialized nurse. She needed him as Nicholas, the answer to all the longing he had roused in her, the culmination of the feelings unfamiliar to the big body that housed a heart that ached for him.

Chapter Eight

The posted hospital schedules gave Samantha the time off she wanted. In a fit of sudden homesickness, she called her mother to let her know she was flying home for a few days. And, as usual, was sorry a few hours after arriving there.

The storms that had plagued her isolated cabin duty with Nicholas followed close behind her, and thunder rolled across the hill country with heavy rains blowing in sheets.

Samantha turned from the window to see Emily curled into the big club chair, small white teeth biting into her lower lip, and remembered somewhat guiltily that while she was enjoying the display put on by the storm, that Emily was terrified.

Smiling at the younger woman, she said, "I need to do some shopping. After this passes, let's go downtown."

Emily's eyes, darker than Samantha's, went over her generous figure and back to her face. "I thought you were going to lose some of that weight before you bought any more clothes. The only place you can buy anything to fit you is that large women's department store, and that's not in the new mall." Her full lips parted in a derisive smile. "There's nothing there that I can use."

"I prefer to go to the mall, Emily, to do some shopping I won't be able to do in Yakima. There's a much better selection in the larger stores here that we don't have." She turned to her mother, catching her studying her proportions with critical eyes. "Would you like to go, Mums?"

"No, you girls go. I'll get dinner ready." She was nice enough to refrain from adding her criticism to Emily's, and Samantha felt a rush of affection for her mother.

The storm diminished and Emily's disposition improved considerably, even if her mouth retained its viciousness. As she drove her small sports car toward the shopping district, she talked about her job as executive secretary in the office of the gas company's president.

"I love being a one-woman office, and Mr. Gower is very generous," she said. "I really don't see how you stand to wait on people all the time, emptying bedpans and listening to old people grumble."

A thrill of anger brought Samantha as near as she had ever come to giving her sister a cutting answer. She took a deep breath, briefly wondering what Emily would say if she told her she had spent the past week with a handsome logger all alone in the wilderness. Not a company president—just an average working guy hurt on the job.

She looked out the car window, grinning at the thought of Emily massaging the big body and fending off big hands that insisted on the "hands-on touch" procedure.

"Old people are not the only ones who get sick, Emily. Illness doesn't discriminate. Just be thankful that you're healthy."

"I take good care of myself," Emily said and sent her a mocking glance. "I don't overeat and I exercise regularly."

She didn't give Emily an answer and was glad when the little sports car whipped into a parking place near the new mall that had opened since the last time she was in San Antonio.

For the next two hours she concentrated on her shopping and followed Emily into the expensive-smelling cosmetics department, watching while her sister debated the pros and cons of the latest perfume products and moisturizers.

"You smell like a baby," she heard Nicholas murmur and her lips parted at the memory of the kisses she shared with him. She wondered if the operation was over, hoping it was.

Sadness took away the smile as she realized she'd never know what happened to him, but one thing for sure, she'd never forget the week that brought work and worry and the love she would have kept for her own had she been allowed.

At dinner that evening, her mother pursued her favorite subject. "Are you dating anyone in particular, Samantha?"

Emily looked up with her kittenish smile and waited for the answer. "I go out with Dr. Jarvis from the hospital. We go camping a lot since I got my new van."

"Camping? Is that what you call dating?" Emily's soft drawl held disdain. "What about dinner and dancing?" Her eyes went over her sister. "Is he as big as you?"

Samantha held her tongue for a moment, then shook her head. "No, I'm quite a bit bigger than he is, so he gives me no trouble. Neither of us cares for dancing."

Her mother frowned. "A regular medical doctor? I've heard they don't make a lot of money unless they specialize in a difficult field of medicine."

Trying to keep her voice milder than she felt, Samantha said, "I'm not looking for anyone rich, Mums. Someone healthy will do." In spite of all her efforts, her words conveyed a harsh criticism of her mother's opinion.

She stood up and began putting the dishes in the dishwasher, leaving her mother and Emily looking after her in astonishment. Samantha never talked back or defended herself to them, usually ignoring any unsavory remarks that came her way just to avoid argument. The straightness of her broad back told the other two in no uncertain terms that they had gone too far this time.

As soon as she was left alone, Samantha dialed the airport and changed her Tuesday morning reservations to Sunday night. She related this information to them the next morning at breakfast and ignored the surprised comments.

With a sigh of relief, she packed her few things and her shopping results and left, feeling nothing but contentment as she watched the lights of Yakima come closer and become a golden carpet beneath the big 727 as it touched the runway and rolled to a stop.

Leo was back on Monday night and interested in the details of her last assignment. One thing about Leo, whatever she did interested him and they could always find a comical angle to laugh at.

"Between the two of us we must have weighed four hundred pounds," she told him, shaking her head. "You wouldn't have believed him, Leo." Her expression softened. "I hope he gets some good care; that leg was a mess."

She looked up. "What do you know about the orthopedic team in Los Angeles?"

He thought a moment. "The last time I read about them, they were exchanging doctors and getting two from Europe supposed to be some of the best bone specialists, but I'd have gone to Chicago if I'd had a choice."

She nodded. "That's what I thought, but arrangements had been made by his company and I wasn't asked." She played with the crust of her bread and looked up to see Leo's dark eyes watching her.

"Did anything else interesting happen?" he asked.

Taking a deep breath, she lifted her head. "Yes. I fell in love with him." She met his glance, smiling, but he could read the sincerity in her voice and see by her face she was no longer teasing.

"And him?"

"You know all patients fall in love with their nurses, Leo," she said, shaking her head. "He was no exception, but there's a catch. He's also engaged to a tall, slim, beautiful, rich woman. I don't know any more adjectives to describe the perfect, but those will do." She looked back at her plate.

His hand covered hers, his long fingers wrapping around it. "Don't underestimate yourself, Samantha. You're beautiful. Not rich, but lovely and warm. I'm sorry you fell for someone already spoken for, but she doesn't outrank you if the man has any sense at all."

She smiled, swallowing over the tightness in her throat. "Thanks, Leo." She straightened. "That's a great place to camp. We'll have to go up there in the spring. Maybe we can get permission to use hookups to that cabin if we can find the owner through the Forestry Service."

Routine came easily for Samantha as she went around renewing acquaintances with extended-stay patients in Young Memorial such as those in the orthopedic ward. Benjy had gone home to wait three months until bone grafts healed, but he would return for more operations. She missed the little rascal and mailed him a card to tell him so.

A cool, wet fall turned into a cold, dry winter, and her memories of Nicholas Jordan retreated to a soft spot in her heart to be taken out when she was alone and relived again.

Just the thought of him brought back the feel of his mouth on hers, his big hands caressing her body. Time helped little to dull her memories, and she wondered if he and Valerie had ever decided they couldn't live without each other. She had no way of checking on him, not even aware of which lumber company employed him.

She could, she supposed, ask Dr. Reston if he had any information on his location, or she could call Seattle to see if she could locate him, but if he worked all over the state as most loggers did, it would take quite a tracing job to find him. And then there was Valerie.

In late February Leo went to New York for training and observation of new techniques in the medical field, and Samantha was left to her own devices on her days off. She worked a double weekend shift, and instead of her usual four days, she had an entire week free.

"Wouldn't you know?" she wrote Leo. "Here I am with all this time off, and you're three thousand miles away. How did we let this happen? Of course, it will be another year before I get this lucky again. I don't know what I'm going to do, but the weather is dry and has warmed up quite a bit, just perfect for camping if you were here." She had watched the newscast earlier and couldn't resist adding, "I hear New York is under blizzard conditions with a foot of snow. Too bad we never learned to ski." She grinned as she visualized Leo's fist shaking at her.

It didn't take long for her to catch up on her laundry, write letters, and clean her room. Saturday morning dawned clear and bright, temperature due to go into the sixties, with a similar five-day forecast that could change with the hour, she knew.

"I can't believe this," she fumed to herself. "Here I am with all this time off, and I'm already bored." She groaned. "Leo, how could you do this to me?"

Making up her mind, she packed her heavy pants and sweaters and insulated jacket against the mountain winds and turned the van toward Rimrock Canyon. As soon as she left the city limits, her spirits lifted. She was one who didn't have to have someone with her, although Leo was as comfortable as an old shoe plus a lot of fun. She missed him as much as she missed Benjy.

At the turnoff to Rimrock, Samantha slowed the van and pulled to the shoulder of the road. She could drive at least five miles up the canyon before she reached the portion still closed because of heavy snows that could come as late as April. Her glance strayed to the narrow stream that was the Naches River as it turned west, musing at the sight as she wondered if the water was running north or south. It always seemed to her to be running uphill.

Pulling the van back on the highway, she passed the turnoff to Rimrock and continued on Route 410 without thinking about where she was going. Just before she came to American River, she turned the van toward Goose Prairie, the direction the faded sign pointed to, taking the gravel road toward the cabin where she had stayed with Nicholas several months before.

Another sign had been added as a warning: Road closed—heavy snows. She drove past it, dodging the deep washes left by rains and melting snows.

An excited thrill started below her ribs, and her breath came a little more quickly as she guided the van around the bends and up the hills, finally coming into sight of the cabin. A big gray van with one wide maroon stripe around it was parked near the doorway, and thin gray smoke trailed from the chimney.

"Damn," she said aloud, slowing her van. "I should have known with the good weather, it would bring everybody out after being shut up all winter."

Hunters, she suspected, and frowned. She hated the forests to be disturbed by loud gunshots, even without thinking about destroying wildlife.

She parked near the big gray van and slid from the seat, glancing around at the quiet serenity, breathing in the unexpectedly dry air.

The door to the cabin opened, and she turned, eyes widening in disbelief. Nicholas stood in the doorway, leaning on a crutch.

He grinned. "Hello, Sam. What took you so long?"

"Nicholas!" She hurried to him, taking in the loss of weight even under the wine-colored jogging suit, the thinness of his face beneath the heavy streaked beard, dark shadows under the blue eyes. She reached out to him, and his right arm extended toward her.

Samantha stared up into his smiling face. "What do you mean what took you so long?"

"I've been here since last night and was hoping you'd show up."

"Why in the world would you expect me?" She smiled up at him, still not quite sure he was there. She shook her head before he could answer. "How did the operation go? What did they say? You can drive with that leg already? Oh, Nicholas."

He laughed. "Wait a minute. Come on inside where I can sit down. I've been wandering around in the woods, and I'm already worn out." He kept her hand in his as they went back inside.

In the dimness of the cabin, she could feel warmth from the stove, and through the door opened into the other room, she saw the brightness of flames in the fireplace.

He turned to face her, drawing her to him. "Oh, Sam, I missed you so. You should never have let me go alone."

He bent his head, and she lifted her face to him. It was as natural as the sun rising over the Cascades—Nicholas with his arms around her, his rough beard, which he had obviously decided to keep, brushing her cheeks before his mouth closed over hers. She stood still against him, breathing in the smell of him, feeling the strength of his arms and body, even though he still leaned on the crutch.

His mouth was on hers briefly, then moved along her jawline to her ear, upward to her temple, across her forehead, and down the straight line of her nose. He kissed the tip and raised his head to smile down at her.

"I dreamed about you all through the operations. That's the only thing that kept me from tearing the place apart." He pulled her to him again, sighing into her hair. "It was awful, Sam. You should have gone with me to hold my hand."

Her arms were around his big body, holding tightly. She rubbed her face on the soft fabric of the warm-up top and put her head back to look up at him.

"Are you all right, now?"

He nodded. "Now that you're here." He straightened, putting his right arm around her. "Let's go in the other room where we can sit down."

He grimaced as he lowered himself into the old club chair, and she knelt by him as his arm came around her shoulders. "Why did you come back here, Nicholas?"

He smoothed the soft hair back from her cheeks. "I

was looking for you, Sam." He tilted her chin. "Why did you come at this time of year?"

"It was on the spur of the moment," she told him and admitted, smiling, "I was looking for you, Nicholas." She ran her fingers down the injured leg. "Do you still have pain?"

"Some, but not much." His big hand moved from her face to her shoulder, pulling her to him. "I didn't know how to get in touch with you. I couldn't even remember the name of the hospital where you worked." He shook his head. "I could have called the company where I worked, I suppose, but they're so nosy. I didn't want anyone to know how much I enjoyed my private nurse even though I was badly hurt."

Leaning away to look into her upturned face, he added, "I must have been a mess for you to handle alone. How did you manage?"

"Aside from broken furniture, crushed ribs, and threats of what to do with the bedpan, you weren't so bad."

He laughed aloud, shaggy head thrown back, and she felt him down to her toes. The laugh shook his big body, and she smiled at the humor she saw in his face. He knew exactly what he had put her through.

She looked around. "Where's Hannibal?"

He grinned at her. "I left her with Noelle. I was afraid she'd get frisky and I wouldn't be able to keep up with her."

"Your family get back in time for the operation?"

"Yes, they were there. I'm sure Foster gave orders not to touch me until he could tell them how to do their job. You'd think I was twelve." He shook his head.

"You were right. The team in Los Angeles was really something. Two of the surgeons were just out of Europe somewhere, and I understand they're experts in the orthopedic field with all the latest techniques. All I know is that everyone seems to think they performed a miracle getting me back together without a transplant." He ruffled her hair. "Are you hungry?"

"Do I get that steak now?" she teased.

"Would you believe I brought steaks for two with me? How certain could I be that you'd find me?" He chuckled again, bringing color to her cheeks and a smile that parted her lips. He bent and kissed her, easing her bright head into the curve of his arm, neither of them noticing as the crutch thumped to the floor beside him.

Samantha thought briefly of Valerie but now was not the time to ask, and she gave herself up to the sweetness that filled her as Nicholas closed long fingers around her throat, his thumb stroking behind her ear. She was kneeling in an awkward position and straightened as he released her.

Breathing hard, she leaned away from him, hearing his breath and feeling the warmth of it on her face. She had to start some kind of conversation.

With her fingers resting on his lips, she asked, "Your shoulder, Nicholas? Did you have any trouble with that?"

"No. You were right. Once they got the bandage and sling off that Dr. Knight had put on and the soreness wore off, I didn't have any problem with it." He grimaced again. "Good thing, too. The leg was enough."

His glance roved over her face, and she touched his

thick beard, rubbing her fingers downward over the wiry blond-streaked mat of hair. He turned so that her fingers moved over his lips. They stared into each other's eyes, hungry for the image they had both dreamed about.

He shook his head. "I still can't believe I have you back." He took her fingers from his mouth and squeezed them against his chest. "Foster asked me if I was having an affair with a man because I kept calling for Sam."

Samantha giggled. "What did you tell him?"

"I told him you were my male nurse he requested."

"Nicholas! Did you ever tell him any different?"

"No." He laughed deep in his throat. "Foster appreciated that and said he hoped he was the size of Rosie Grier."

She bit her lip and felt the color come into her face. "Not quite." Emily would love that comparison.

"Sam. I didn't mean to embarrass you." He looked her over, her big body leaning awkwardly over the chair arm close to him. "Why do you consider yourself too big? You don't come anywhere close to being my size." He added with a smile that had grown tender, his eyes half closed as he looked down at her. "Thank goodness, I might add."

She stood up and moved away from him toward the fireplace. "Can you walk without the crutch?" she asked, trying to get away from personalities.

"Yes, but when I get tired I have to use it. That leg sometimes feels like it has hot coals inside it, all of them trying to escape through my ankle."

"When do you go back for therapy?"

"I've just got out of a week of it, and I have to be back in ten days." He was watching her as she put another log on the fire from the stack he had brought in. "How long before you have to report back to the hospital?"

She smiled over her shoulder. "A week."

Immediately she wished she had told him she had to be back on Monday. Then she could have left before he was aware of her feelings. But from the greeting she gave him, he must guess she was kind of glad to see him—to put it very mildly.

"What's happened with you since October?" he asked finally.

"The usual routine. I did fly home to San Antonio for a few days after I left my duty here with you." She didn't feel any inclination to go into detail about her shortened visit.

"I still have almost all the same patients I had back then, with the exception of Benjamin Carter." She laughed. "He gives me as much trouble as you did, although he isn't quite as big as you."

He frowned. "Is he my competition?"

Her breath exhaled sharply. "Competition for what?"

"I consider you my own private nurse, Sam," he said, "and I don't want anyone else with that claim."

The smile he sent her way did strange things to her blood pressure and her body trembled as though he touched a sensitive spot.

"Is he?" he insisted.

Her laugh was shaky as she tried to control her need to go to him and put her head in his lap.

"Don't you remember my story about Benjy and his

escapes from his bed? He's just special to me, that's all."

He frowned a little. "Vaguely. A lot of what went on seems a bit like a dream, Sam. Did he recover enough to leave for good?"

She sobered, shaking her head. "No. They haven't found the cause of the calcium leakage, and until they do, Benjy will spend more time in the hospital than anywhere else."

"Then you're right; I really am lucky."

"Yes, Nicholas. Very lucky."

His eyes left her face to stare at the bright fire, and when he looked back at her, they were dreamy. Without a word he held out his hand to her, and she went to him, sitting on the floor and leaning against his chair.

His hand dropped to her shoulder and they sat quietly. He pulled her head closer until it rested on his leg, and she felt him relax a little in the chair. The crackling of the fire they both watched was the only sound in the room.

"Are you tired?" she asked.

"Yes."

She sat up. "You should take a nap."

He grinned down at her. "Always the nurse. I think I'll take you home with me to take care of me."

"You can't afford me," she told him lightly, getting to her feet. "I'm sure the lumber company feels they've paid me enough."

"I wouldn't worry about the lumber company's finances, Sam," he said idly. "Don't you think they owe their employees something?"

"Sure, but not a private nurse after you're well and able to rough it in a cabin in the wilderness."

"Well, look at it this way. If it hadn't been for them, I wouldn't have been hurt." He reached for her hand. "But then I never would have met you."

"I never did tell Valerie about your philandering habits," she said over the sudden racing of her pulse. "Has anyone filled her in on that aspect of your character?"

He laughed. "She knows me pretty well, I guess." He squeezed her fingers lightly and released them. "I'm not as tired as I'm hungry. What say we try those steaks?"

"Can you cook?"

"Certainly. Believe me, Josephine and Foster made sure Noelle and I could do anything that would help us survive. Cooking was one of them."

"I must meet those parents of yours, Nicholas. They sound marvelous."

The chuckle was deep in his chest and Samantha loved the sound. "They're wonderful. Every set of parents should be identical to them."

But they aren't, she thought silently and handed the crutch to him, staying well out of his reach as they started toward the kitchen. Self-discipline had to start somewhere.

"You can check out the things I brought and tell me what you need from the pantry," he said.

Opening the small refrigerator, she peered inside. Two huge T-bone steaks lapped over the edge of a platter. Hunks of cheese were wrapped in clear wrap; ingredients for fresh salad were in the crisper. She looked over her shoulder at him. "Josephine taught you to shop, too?"

"I can even empty bedpans if I have to," he assured her.

Samantha shook with laughter. "Let's hope it doesn't come to that."

Busy with getting everything out of the refrigerator and reaching for a bowl from the cabinet, she turned to find his eyes going over her figure. She blushed as he smiled at her, but he said nothing as she started cutting the vegetables for the salad.

He worked, too, setting the table; and as she used a dish and put it aside, he washed it, leaning against the sink for support. Without appearing to do so, she watched his movements. He favored the left leg, careful not to bump against the cabinets.

As he left the sink, she asked, "You want your steak medium rare?"

"Is there any other way?" he countered.

"Suppose not," she said, busy rubbing cracked peppers into the tender meat. She looked at the bottle of steak sauce nearby. "You wouldn't really put that stuff on this piece of meat, would you?"

"I thought you might," he said.

"How could you think that, Nicholas?" she asked, horror mirrored on her face.

He was quiet for an instant before he said, "I don't know enough about you, Sam." When she didn't answer him, he went on. "I plan to remedy that while you're here."

Keeping her face turned away from him, she said, "I can fill in the gaps for you." When he didn't say anything, she went on, "We played twenty questions before."

"Yes, but you imparted very little useful information," he reminded her.

"Well, if I had, you'd have forgotten it by now."

"You may be right. I wasn't exactly clearheaded." He continued to watch as she mixed the salad. "Shame. That must have been the week that was."

"Yes, I should have had my recorder going." She laughed lightly. "You wouldn't believe some of the stuff even if I told you."

The smell of the steaks soon filled the room, and Samantha was busy concentrating to get them cooked just right. He opened a can of mushrooms and heated them in plenty of butter, placing them on the back of the stove to keep warm as he put out the salad dressing and took a bottle of wine from one of the crispers.

He grinned at her surprised look. "I told you I was expecting you. You don't really think I'd drink alone, do you?"

A few minutes later they sat down at the small table, eyeing the results of their combined efforts with appreciation. Hungry, they concentrated on eating.

He sighed aloud. "Just the way I pictured it," he said.

She laughed, taking a sip of the wine. "Not me. I was looking forward to a can of Vienna sausage."

He shook his head. "I can't stand the stuff."

"Neither can I, but it keeps well and you don't have to cook, a disaster for one person."

"Aren't you afraid to camp alone way off up here, Sam?"

"No. I'm big enough to take care of myself."

His voice soft, he said, "You're a woman, and a woman should never camp alone."

"Why, Nicholas, don't tell me you still believe a woman should be taken care of?"

"Yes," he said flatly. "I think a woman should be taken care of."

She stared at him. "I don't believe what I'm hearing. A modern man who goes by the old rules."

"Not all of them," he said, his eyes going from her face down the well-filled sweater, to her hands holding the fork poised over her plate.

"What does that mean?" she asked, her breath suddenly short.

His smile enclosed her in its intimacy. "My parents would never have spent a week together in an isolated cabin before they were married."

The heat consumed her body, starting with flames in her cheeks, and she looked at her plate, unable to meet his eyes. Nicholas had the capability to turn her into a speechless schoolgirl; somehow to make her think she could be loved the same as a slender woman, the same as Valerie or Emily.

They finished the delicious meal, but she was aware of his eyes following her as she moved to clear the table and make coffee on the top of the stove. He washed the dishes as she dried them and put them away, stretching to replace them on the high cabinet shelves. She turned away from hanging the dishcloth on a nail near the stove to find herself in his arms.

Samantha stood still as he lowered his face to hers, his lips skimming her cheek before resting on hers. Big hands slid up and down on her arms from elbows to underarms, then moved downward to form caressing brackets over her breasts, his palms gently rubbing back and forth.

He raised his head, and she sighed, leaning on him. In the past months she had convinced herself that her feeling for Nicholas was sympathy, coupled with the need they shared to be close to each other as they fought his problems and those of nature. She was wrong to think it was a superficial feeling, one that she would forget even if it took time. This was the one love of her lifetime. Wouldn't you know she'd pick the most unavailable—and unforgettable—man of all time.

"Coffee's ready," she said.

He let her go and she fixed their cups and started into the other room, looking back over her shoulder at him. Smiling, he followed her.

As he sat in the club chair, she handed him a cup and went to sit on the floor near the fireplace, placing her cup on the hearth. She poked absently at the fire and added a log from her sitting position.

"Did you bring cards?" he asked.

"Yes, as a matter of fact." It was her turn to grin. "Did you bring a book by your favorite author?"

"It's in the van," he said, laughing. "You want to read to me?"

"No, thanks. I have a whodunit you can listen to."

He put up his hand. "Spare me. The butler is always guilty."

They were quiet for a time, then he said, "You can sleep on the bunk. I brought my sleeping bag."

Her stomach flipped, but she asked in a normal

voice, "Are you ready for bed? Do you still take medication?"

"Yes. No," he said.

Sticking with a safe subject, she asked, "You mean you don't have to take anything for pain?"

"Not often."

She shook her head. "Nicholas, don't tell me you're one of those brave souls that refuses medicine because you think it's a weakness."

"Not me," he said. "I can't stand pain."

"Good," she told him, taking their cups, heading for the kitchen. "If anything gets on my nerves, it's these people who think they have to be big and brave when it comes to suffering. That's what the medical profession is for, so I think it should be used."

When she returned to the bedroom, his chin was propped on one big hand as he stared into the fire. He looked up to grin at her.

"My thigh aches like crazy. I need a massage."

"Does this come under the heading of 'other duties as assigned'?"

"I'd rather you consider it a pleasure."

She looked down at him, and he continued to stare up, the smile fading from his face. He held out his hand, and she knelt beside him, kissing his hairy cheek before she settled on the floor by the chair.

His arm remained around her shoulders, thumbs sliding absently over the curving slope down her arm. She didn't know who made the first move, but as their eyes met and held, he whispered her name, a mere breath of a question.

Samantha got up and removed the blankets from the

bunk where she had cared for him that memorable week many months ago and spread them near the fire, watching as he moved to join her, conscious of the care he took as he straightened his leg in front of him.

He reached for her and they lay back together, his mouth hungrily searching for hers. Her arms encircled his hard-muscled body she had long since found had little excess fat on it.

Lying stretched alongside him, she felt dwarfed by his long arms holding her as though she were small and dainty.

"Honey," he whispered. "Sam." He lay back, and she raised up enough to lean over him, her hands at the elastic waist of his jogging suit. He lifted his hips, and she didn't miss the quick bite on his lips as she pushed the knit fabric downward, leaving thick thighs exposed in the warm firelight.

She sat up and moved so she could reach his left leg and, without speaking, began massaging, her strong fingers pressing into the muscles. He made no sound as she worked her way to his ankle, feeling for tenderness. Taking his right foot in her hand, she rubbed upward to his thigh, tensed beneath her hands.

He caught her shoulders, pulling her up to him, his hands moving quickly to help remove her clothing. She tried to roll away from him, but he held her.

"I'm afraid I'll hurt you," she whispered.

"No, you won't hurt me; you'll love me," he murmured. "Darling."

With a depth of tenderness Samantha didn't know existed, Nicholas took her heart along with her body, manipulating them until their sighs mingled and they lay trembling in the dying firelight.

They walked through the woods, their feet crackling the dry leaves. Winter starlings chattered at them, frightened at the invasion of their domain. Circling back to the yard, they stopped to get an armful of wood to take inside.

"Whose cabin is that?" she asked.

"I got the key from the forest ranger at the post near American River. I guess they're caretakers for the property," he said, slipping his arm around her as they put the wood in the corner.

"Probably," she agreed, her voice dreamy.

He grinned at her and led her into the bedroom. "Come into my parlor, my lovely," he said.

She raised her eyebrows. "I sense a seduction scene."

"Good. I'll cooperate." He laughed down at her.

Samantha moved against him as they lay on the blankets. Her fingers slid across his mouth to his hairy cheek, and he trembled as he stroked her hip with just the tips of his fingers.

He was lying on his right side and, carefully, she drew her leg up between his, tilting her head back on the pillow to watch him. His eyes were closed.

"Are you all right?" she asked.

He moved his head slightly to place his mouth over hers, kissing her with tiny kisses, and with his lips touching hers, whispered, "I will be in a moment."

His hand slid over her rounded hips and fitted behind her, pressing the tips of his fingers into her flesh. Each pinpoint of pressure touched a nerve that quivered into a response so intense she was forced to open her eyes, searching for reassurance from him. She found it in the fiery blue gaze that veiled behind heavy lashes as he kissed her, tongue plundering easily inside her mouth.

It was her moan she heard and his crying her name as he took possession of her, withholding nothing, giving everything.

If I could have one day that lasts forever, it would be today, she thought, as she gave herself to him and they shared the love she had only dreamed of before.

Samantha found a jar of popcorn in the pantry and used the big iron skillet with margarine to pop corn, which they ate as they sat in front of the fireplace.

"This is exactly what I shouldn't be eating," she said, licking her fingers.

"Why?" he asked, popping another puffy kernel into her mouth.

"Look at me and ask that question. How can anyone love a mass of flesh like this?" Startled at her own question, she met the bright blue of his eyes.

"Do you measure love by size, Sam?" he asked quietly.

A vision of Valerie came before her, and she remembered his sister's name, Noelle, surely a tiny miniature of her brother with a name like Noelle. She envisioned Emily with her long slender body, sensuous in any outfit as compared to her own larger-than-life-size proportions. Nicholas could speak of love, but he would leave her very soon, returning to the woman who carried a figure more acceptable to society.

She swallowed. "I've never thought about measuring it," she said. "If it weighs as much as I do, it's too heavy, though." She rose and took his empty bowl from him, carrying it to the kitchen.

When Samantha returned to the room, he was staring into the fire, his left leg stretched in front of him.

"Do you want me to massage your leg?"

Nicholas looked up at her. "I want to hold you more than anything else I can think of." She sat beside him, and he encircled her body with a long arm, pulling her back on the blanket with him.

They lay quietly, the only movement his hands touching her hair, fingers pressing her earlobe, his forefinger following the hollow of her throat down to the deep cleft separating her breasts. Her bra fastened in front, and he released it, whispering, "I like that." He drew in a sharp breath as his hand closed over the firm mound of flesh exposed to his touch.

"Sweetheart," he murmured and nestled closer to place his lips in the warm valley. Her fingers tangled in his hair, then gently stroked the thickness, bringing her hand under his jaw to hold him there.

Dreamily she pressed closer as his lips closed over the wide brown peak near his mouth, holding it captive, wrapping his tongue around its hardness.

She gasped as he released it, looking down into her wide eyes.

"You're the sweetest armful I've ever held," he said, pushing her easily until she lay on her back.

Neither of them thought of his injured leg as they tasted the sweetness of the love created between them.

They said good-bye on Thursday afternoon. He held her close and said, "You don't know what this week has meant to me, Sam. I don't have to tell you I wish you could go back with me to Seattle." He kissed her on the mouth. "Can I call you next week?"

"Yes," she said, knowing she should mention Valerie. She gave him her dormitory number.

"I'll give you the address where I'll be the next couple of months when I call you. I'm not sure right now."

"Take care," she told him, pulling away so he couldn't see her straining to hold back tears. She knew the uncertainty of lumbermen's living quarters and that they moved frequently according to contracts their company received, and understood the need to wait for a new address.

She climbed into the van and waved before turning down the narrow trail toward Route 410 and Yakima.

Chapter Nine

The quiet halls of the hospital echoed with her footsteps as Samantha went about checking her patients in the early morning hours. Her mind for once was not on their welfare but tied in knots as she worked at her own problem.

The calendar had never lied to her, and she knew with certainty that she was pregnant. Had known for some time. For weeks her body had felt alive and glowing, her eyes shining with some kind of inner light, and she hadn't really needed the calendar to confirm her suspicions. Her week with Nicholas was unforgettable in the sweetness of the love they had shared, and now there would be a memory lasting forever. Her wish to keep that one day forever had been granted.

Thoughts churned around inside of her, trying to clear themselves of the mixture of excitement and deep-down fright at the thought of having a baby, being unmarried, and having the father engaged to another woman, perhaps already married, unaware that she was pregnant.

Would he want to know? Nicholas would never think

of pregnancy; most men today concluded women knew how to take care of themselves. Samantha knew—she had never given any thought that she needed any precautions. She had few propositions.

Leo was her friend and they shared only friendship and fun. With Nicholas she shared everything she owned. He had been fair—he had given equally, except for his heart, which she knew was already taken. She didn't blame him for her predicament.

The halls became busier as it neared shift-changing time, and she finished her reports and put away leftover supplies. Exchanging morning greetings with her relief, she went through the back hall toward the dormitory, glancing at the closed conference room door. Where all her troubles had started. Where the most happiness she had ever known began.

Easing her big body between the sheets, she lay staring at the ceiling, but it gave her no answers to what she must do.

Awake a few hours later, Samantha made up her mind and went to the small desk in the corner of the room. When she completed the letter to Nicholas, she addressed it to the lumber company that originally requested the male nurse, to the only address they had on file. It had been six weeks since Nicholas promised to call her, and she had heard nothing from him. The lumber company was her only link.

As days passed and she heard nothing, her doubts increased, and she concluded that Nicholas had no intention of contacting her. The emptiness inside her was lined with a throbbing ache with the realization that she had meant little to him.

The recriminations she leveled at herself for being so gullible as to think a man like Nicholas Jordan could love her brought only a derisive smile to her mouth. Two weeks later, her letter was returned with the notation: Addressee unknown; return to sender.

Familiar routine was her only outlet for her feelings, and she worked, her mind going in all directions without finding a solution. Abortion was out of the question. Her mouth twisted as she thought of going to her mother for support. Emily would have a field day with the idea that her *big* sister was pregnant without benefit of husband.

"Who in the world would she know that intimately?" she could almost hear Emily drawl. "One bed isn't big enough for her, much less two people."

Blankets on the floor were big enough to hold two people, and neither had noticed it wasn't a comfortable bed. Neither had noticed anything except the feelings they shared. It was only the feelings that Nicholas shared; he wasn't interested in a follow-up.

Nor could she really blame him. She was old enough to have more sense than to become involved with an almost-stranger. No, Nicholas had never been a stranger. She had loved him almost from the beginning, but that was still no reason to have landed blindly into this predicament.

Why in the world had she gone back to the cabin?

"I was waiting for you, Sam." he had said.

It went without saying that her decision to go back hadn't really been her choice at all. Nicholas wanted her to return, and she did.

Engrossed in her misery, she felt the time slip away

and realized Leo was due back from his temporary duty in New York. With rare enthusiasm he told her about the new procedures he had studied and that he was getting ready to write a proposal for a similar program at Young Memorial.

"We'll need good nurses, Samantha, and I want you to head the team. How about taking a leave of absence from the orthopedics ward and going with us to Los Angeles for six months?"

She looked across at him, stirring her coffee absently. "I've already put in for a leave of absence, Leo."

Startled, he stared at her. "How did you know I'd ask?"

She shook her head. "I didn't. I'm going to San Antonio to take care of my mother for a while."

"What happened?"

It was hard to lie to Leo, but she took a deep breath, repeating to him what she had told Dr. Reston. "She needs me there to help her since the operation. Emily isn't much good in a sickroom."

Samantha evaded the truth, but the last statement was certainly a fact. Sick people were treated like contagious diseases by Emily. Her mother's operation was only the removal of bunions, but it sufficed as a cause she could relate to Leo and Dr. Reston.

They didn't need to know that should her mother ever really need her, she would see to it that she was taken care of, but she would never do it personally. They couldn't be around each other many hours before their personalities clashed, and they'd last about two days before her mother would be sicker than ever and Samantha would be near a nervous breakdown.

But for now she used her mother as her excuse for requesting six months' leave of absence from the hospital to have her baby.

Her request was granted, and she had a brief sense of regret at lying to Dr. Reston when he was instantly sympathetic.

"Of course, Miss Bridges. We'll certainly miss you here, but by all means take the time to care for your mother." He smiled. "At least we here at Young know she's in good hands."

He picked up his usual pencil to twist in his hands. "By the way, a letter of commendation will go into your file for the way you handled the logger patient last fall. They were most happy with your services."

He opened his desk drawer. "I was asked to give you this, along with the utmost thanks from Mr. Jordan's employer." He handed her a check.

She looked at the check, her heart beating rapidly as she scanned it for an address. It was drawn on a bank in Seattle, and she knew how much chance she had of getting information from them.

Swallowing over her disappointment, she asked, "Whom did you finally hear from? Did Mr. Jordan write to let you know how he was doing after the operation?" She held her breath.

He shook his head. "The lumber company's administrative office in Seattle wrote the letter." He picked up an envelope and handed it to her. The return address was the one to which she had addressed her letter telling Nicholas about the baby.

Samantha could only conclude that Nicholas didn't wish any further contact with her. Nodding, she rose to go. "Thank you, Dr. Reston. I'll write you when I know how long I'll be."

The trembling in her legs lasted the rest of the day, and now as she sat with Leo, she felt the familiar tightening in her chest. Lies didn't come easily for her at any time, and to lie to Leo hurt her deeply.

As the weeks passed, she could feel life within her. The pain persisted each time she thought of Nicholas who had disappeared without a backward glance. Just to walk away and not look back...

Her body showed no signs of her pregnancy, and aside from vitamins and a mild fluid pill, she didn't change her routine at all.

Two months before the baby was due, she started her leave of absence and moved from the dormitory to a small cottage she found on the southwest side of town where she wouldn't be likely to run into anyone from the hospital.

A new neighbor recommended a doctor nearby who delivered his patients' babies at a small clinic rather than in the hospital. He gave her a clean bill of health when he examined her, with only a mild caution. "Don't gain any more weight, Mrs. Bridges," he told her. "Your doctor should have had you on a stricter diet, but at least your blood pressure is normal. Keep it that way."

There were no questions about her moving into the area when her logger husband took a job; no one thought it strange she had no family around since the state of Washington was filled with mobile families living apart under strained economic conditions.

Keeping the small cottage neat and walking a lot kept

her busy during the day, but at night she twisted in anguish as the time drew near for the baby to be born. Nicholas came into her thoughts and lingered there, reminding her of his touch and remembered conversations so precious to her.

For a time, Samantha was convinced he felt more than passing desire for her, but as weeks and months passed and she didn't hear anything from him, she concluded that she had been at the right place at the wrong time, and she alone would pay for it.

Nicole Bridges made her entrance into the world nearly a month earlier than predicted on a lovely late October morning, almost a year to the day from the time Nicholas Jordan entered her mother's life. Samantha smiled as she touched the tiny features. Her well-shaped head was covered with dark-blond fuzz, and the eyes that opened so seldom were almost black.

Ten days after her birth, Nicole came home to the cottage, where her mother placed her in the crib she had bought at a yard sale and stripped down and painted creamy white. The small bedroom, not much bigger than a closet, had been painted creamy white on three walls, and one wall had been covered with wallpaper of nursery characters, a riot in pale yellows, greens, and orchid. Just right for a dainty little girl.

Odd how such a tiny being could occupy twenty-four hours of every day, but Samantha was so busy she found little time to think about her new role in life. Nicholas retreated in her thoughts during her busy day, but as Nicole grew, she changed and began to resemble the man who was her father.

The black eyes became a brilliant blue; her hair was blond with darker streaks, a pixie copy of her father's shaggy head. Her fingers grew long and slim like her mother's.

"You have beautiful hands, Sam," she heard Nicholas say as she washed the baby-soft hands. She blinked away the tears she couldn't afford to have fall and lifted Nicole into her arms, wrapping a towel round her firm little body.

"You smell like a baby." She gave up trying to forget him. As long as Nicole lived, she would have a part of Nicholas.

With Nicole tucked into her crib sound asleep, she picked up the morning paper and sat down with her one cup of coffee she allowed herself. The caffeine wasn't good for a baby, and as long as she was nursing her, she would be careful of her diet.

Samantha didn't lose much weight after the baby's birth, but she firmed down. Her long walks pushing the baby in the carriage had brought tightness to her body.

Absently she scanned the movie columns. Keeping up with what was being shown in the movies was a pastime she enjoyed, though she seldom went to see them. She had watched movie awards sometimes on the television in the lounge at Young Memorial and recognized names, even if she didn't remember faces of actresses and actors.

In the column alongside the movie listings, she read a review of the film about the man who had won custody of his son when he and his wife divorced.

"Men love their children, too," he said. "It's only fair we get positive exposure reflecting this."

Placing the paper aside, she leaned over the table, her head in her hands. If Nicholas knew about Nicole, would he care? Would he feel cheated not having seen her when she was a baby?

Samantha stood up, moving automatically about her daily routine. When she first discovered she was pregnant, she fought resentment; later she fought loneliness when she made her decision to have the baby alone. It was panic she fought when the letter was returned to her with the notation "addressee unknown."

But had she been able to reach Nicholas, would he have reacted differently? She didn't know the answer to that.

Suddenly she very much wanted him to know he had a daughter. Even if he couldn't accept it, he should at least know he was a father. There had to be a way to locate him, perhaps using a private detective.

Picking up the paper, she folded it again, and her eyes went over the front page of the business section, scanning the blurred pictures.

"Lumber executives attend foreign rights exchange seminar." Absently she read on. "Yarmouth Lumber executives meet with foreign representatives from Japan, Denmark, and Germany to discuss..."

Yarmouth Lumber Company. The address to which she had sent the letter for Nicholas. She stared at the lines of print. The seminar was being held in Seattle where the headquarters for the company was located.

If Nicholas had ever worked for them, someone at that meeting should know him or his whereabouts. He should know about Nicole. She was so beautiful that it would be shameful to deny him the privilege of seeing her at least once. If she did find him, Nicholas could then make the decision of whether he wished to acknowledge she was his. She would have done her part at least.

Nicole was almost four months old, and Samantha had only one more month before her leave of absence from the hospital was up. The thought of leaving the baby with someone else wasn't pleasant, but she had to work to support them. Her prudent nature enabled them to live well, but her savings wouldn't last much longer at the price of everything today. The bonus check she received from the lumber company where Nicholas had worked had been put aside, but she would use it if it became necessary.

After two days of indecision, she resolutely lifted her chin, packed Nicole into the van, and drove toward Seattle without the slightest idea of how or whether she would find Nicholas. If she didn't, she could accept the fact she had tried, denying to herself all the time that he could have found her had he wanted to.

Less than three hours after leaving home, Samantha drove into the city limits of Seattle, a city of half a million people. At a service station she filled the van with gas and purchased a detailed city map. Nicole was asleep, and her mother smiled at the cherubic face, lips pursed searching for her lunch. Later, she promised, opening the map to find her present location.

She cringed at the intersecting lines of the map. How on earth did anyone find their way around in a place like this? Especially someone from a small town like Yakima.

Sighing, Samantha folded the map and looked around.

There was a phone booth near the corner, and she pulled away from the gas station and parked nearby. In the business section of the telephone book, she located Yarmouth Lumber Company and, before she could change her mind, dialed the number.

"Executive Suite, Yarmouth," a pleasant voice answered.

"Yes," she said distinctly into the phone over her tremulous heartbeat. "Do you have the home address of Mr. Nicholas Jordan, please?"

"One moment." The voice receded and came back. "That address is Orleandro Circle, ma'am."

Shocked at the ease with which she had received the address, Samantha hesitated, "Do you have a telephone number?"

"That number is unlisted. I'm sorry."

Yes, of course, she thought as she hung up. Walking slowly back to the van, she stood staring at the tiny miniature of Nicholas Jordan waving well-formed hands in the air as she caught at dust particles.

Unfolding the map once more, she looked for Orleandro Circle, finding it way out on the north side, miles from the city limits. She went back into the gas station to ask directions.

The attendant frowned "Orleandro Circle?" He turned to another man standing nearby. "Isn't that the area past Yarmouth Lumber near the lake?"

"Yeah," the other man replied. "It's at least fifteen miles from here." He pointed. "Get back on the beltway and take exit fifteen. You'll come out on Highway 99. When you pass the lumber company, it's still about five miles. Big place. You can't miss it."

Thanking him, she returned to the van, climbing up into the seat, checking Nicole automatically. As she re-entered the beltway, she let her thoughts run helter-skelter through her mind, wondering what she was about to find at Orleandro Circle. A big place, he said.

Must be one of those new subdivisions that spread all over creation, tearing up what remaining unsettled property there was near a big city.

Exiting at ramp fifteen, Samantha drew deep breaths to still the trembling inside, daring to hope she would find Nicholas at the end of the specified miles—and afraid she would.

Too soon she passed Yarmouth Lumber, slowing to take in the sprawling modern complex. Lumber had made fortunes in the northwestern state, and Yarmouth was no exception; the owners must be million-aires judging by the size of the place.

Beside her, the baby was sleeping again. She smiled. Nicole was such a good, happy baby, and had never given her any trouble with colic or mixing days with nights to interrupt sleep.

Outside the city limits, the road curved and began to climb, and she looked for signs that would show the address she looked for. To her right a high rock wall protected the property inside for blocks and she wondered what lay beyond it. Could be a hospital. It was certainly big enough and was a quiet, sparsely occupied area, an ideal place for one.

Samantha came upon the gate suddenly, which sat back from the road, up a steep incline. Over the heavy wrought-iron gate was the name: Orleandro Circle. Behind the gate stood a uniformed guard.

A private, restricted residential area. Well, she should have known it wouldn't be easy.

Pulling the van to the side of the road into a turn-around area, she stopped, staring at the scene in front of her.

The road wound back from the gate and disappeared through a row of tall junipers, thick and green. Her eyes returned to the man who stood near a gazebo-type building just inside the gate, watching her.

"Well, Nicole, your mother made a wrong turn some-where down the line." Certainly this was not where Nicholas lived. There must have been two people with that name if this was the only Orleandro Circle in Seattle. Not many loggers could afford to live behind a guarded gate on a private estate, even with all the overtime they put in and counting isolated duty, too.

Samantha sighed and her shoulders slumped, suddenly tired with the letdown of disappointment.

The guard walked to within a few feet of the gate, and it opened automatically. "Can I help you ma'am?" he called.

Glancing at Nicole to see she was still asleep, she opened the door of the van and stepped down, taking a few steps toward him before she answered.

"I guess I'm at the wrong address," she said. "I was looking for the Jordan place."

He nodded. "Were you looking for Foster or Nick?"

The sound of the names shocked her, and she didn't answer him for a moment. He went on. "Perhaps you were looking for Mrs. Jordan or her daughter Noelle?" His eyes went over her curiously, and she returned the look.

He was almost as big as Nicholas, wide shoulders straight in the tailored light blue uniform, and he wore a hat that sported enough braid to resemble an army general's decorations. A gun was strapped at his waist.

She swallowed and shook her head. "I... No, the man I'm looking for is a logger I met sometime ago when he was fighting a fire between here and Yakima. He was hurt."

The man grinned. "That would be Nick," he said.

She never had called him Nick, preferring the romantic sounding Nicholas, and Nicholas he remained until the last time she saw him and always that way in her thoughts.

"Is Nick expecting you?" he asked when she couldn't find her voice.

"No."

"Noelle?" he asked, frowning now.

"I'm looking for my baby's father," she wanted to say, but no words came.

The guard looked from her to the van parked a few yards away, and she could see suspicion beginning to show in his close observation of her.

She wet her lips. "I have the wrong place," she said, turning away from him, her glance going once more down the winding drive that disappeared through the trees. There was no sign of houses or buildings on the spacious grounds, generously sprinkled with flower beds and carefully trimmed shrubs. The deep green velvet of the lawn was an unending carpet that spread away from the road and reached into the vastness, seemingly without end.

As she gazed at the wide expanse, a figure suddenly

appeared, rounding the curve in the driveway, trotting toward the gate. There was no denying the identification of the golden figure coming toward her with the lolling, oddly marked tongue Nicholas called flowered.

Hannibal. The boxy head lifted, and she slowed at the sight of Samantha, emitting a low growl before speeding up, bounding toward her in what would have been an alert move in any other dog.

"Hannibal!" The guard shouted as the dog moved past him at a pace she wouldn't have believed.

The fastest she had ever seen her move was when she relaxed and dropped in her tracks, all wrinkles following suit. Samantha smiled in spite of her frozen astonishment as the dog reached her, standing on hind legs to place broad paws in the hands Samantha extended just in time to keep from going down with the force of the greeting.

Beyond a reasonable doubt, Nicholas lived somewhere in the area. There was only one Hannibal.

The guard reached them, pulling Hannibal back from her. "I'm sorry, miss. I didn't know she was anywhere around. Did she hurt you?"

"No." She knelt in front of the dog, scratching behind the short, pointed ears.

"She seems to know you," he said, his expression puzzled.

"Yes, we've met," she said, still rubbing the dog who sat on her haunches, pointed eyes almost closed, panting in ecstasy as Samantha continued to scratch her.

The guard continued to watch her as she stayed a moment more to pacify the golden animal. "Nick isn't at home today, but I expect him back for the weekend if you'd care to leave a message," he said when she didn't explain her acquaintance with Hannibal.

Murmuring to the dog, she stood up, spreading her palms over the pale blue denim skirt she wore, tucking the white silk blouse deeper beneath the waistband.

Her eyes went over the landscape once more before she smiled at the guard. "No, thank you. I'll come back some other time," she said, turning back to the van. This Nicholas Jordan wouldn't welcome Samantha Bridges, nurse or lover, to an estate such as Orleandro Circle.

There was a mistake somewhere in her conclusions that Nicholas might want to know he had a daughter, a case of greatly mistaken identity caught somewhere between a giant-sized logger and a rich, successful businessman. Her mistake.

As she reached to open the door of the van, a demanding "woof" brought her attention back to Hannibal. Without turning, she said, "Go home, Hannibal. Where were you when I needed you for protection?"

She turned the handle on the door and waited as Hannibal sat, short tail thumping the cement of the drive, looking expectantly toward the windows of the van.

"Want to see your master's creation?" she asked, opening the door and standing aside as the dog leaped easily into the seat, sniffing the quiet bundle lying there. A tiny hand waved in the air and an unmistakable chortle came from Nicole as the animal quietly went over her face and soft down of shaggy hair with her flowered tongue.

Hannibal turned, eyeing Samantha with something like a new respect, and went back to watching the baby. She looked around as the guard came to stand near her elbow.

"I'll be darned," he said. "I've never known her to take up with anyone like this before. She isn't too crazy about Noelle's kids."

Samantha laughed. "She wants all the attention herself and doesn't care to share it with anyone else."

He grinned, his eyes still on the two in the front seat of the van. "You could be right. Nick spoils her rotten and so does Noelle."

Perhaps Nicholas doesn't like children either, she thought as she waited for the guard to retrieve the dog from her van and hold the door for her to climb into it. Hannibal strained to pull away from him, but she was no match for the big guard's strength.

Samantha rolled the window down and said, "Thanks."

"Do you want to leave a message for Nick?"

With one more look at the gate with the electronic lock on it and the dog straining to get away from the guard, she said, "No, it isn't important."

Checking the baby to see she had drifted off to sleep again after Hannibal's inspection, Samantha backed the van up a little to allow herself plenty of room to turn around and pulled back onto the road that had led her to Orleandro Circle.

She hardly saw the white line down the center, didn't see any of the surrounding area, everything vanishing from her sight as she tried to take in what she had just learned.

To her, Nicholas was a logger, hurt in a firefighting accident, needing a male nurse to care for him until he could be moved to a place to have the operations necessary to heal the mangled leg. He was a logger who had returned to the place a nurse had cared for him to find her there, too, loving him as she had months before when he barely knew she was in the world.

His kisses during his semiconscious state had meant something to her, but she had almost succeeded in putting them down as the patient-loves-nurse syndrome she was accustomed to seeing. Almost.

Evidently she had hoped it was as different for him as it was for her. It was. He had returned to the scene of the crime to satisfy his curiosity about a female nurse who'd care for someone in such an extraordinary fashion. Ordinary curiosity.

Her vision blurred and she slowed, pulling to the side of the road to stop, hands clenching and unclenching on the wheel as she stared at the bright sunlight on the hood of the van.

A car came around the curve and sped past her, its powerful motor making less noise than the tires on the pavement. The sudden squeal of rubber on cement brought her sharply back to the present.

She brushed her hand across her cheek, and it came away wet. Taking the corner of Nicole's blanket, she dried the tears and started the van.

The door on her side was yanked violently open, and she cried out at a giant-sized figure that loomed in its place. Nicholas stared at her, disbelief written in the blue eyes.

"Sam!" he said, his voice husky. He reached for her,

pulling her from the van. "Sam!" He searched her face with fierce blue eyes, his lips moving without uttering a sound. He groaned aloud, gathering her close to him, long arms wrapped around her, having no trouble reaching all the way across her back to lock his hands behind her.

His mouth was pressed to her hair, and he rocked her gently back and forth, murmuring her name over and over. She couldn't move, couldn't speak, and so she stood within the circle of his arms, waiting.

After what seemed a long time, he raised his head, bringing her chin up as he did so, to look down into her tear-wet eyes. His thumb caressed her lips, his eyes went over her face, feature by feature.

"Where did you come from?" His arms tightened. "I've looked and waited for you. Oh, Sam!"

Bright blue eyes stared down into hazel-green ones, long lashes darkened with tears. She swallowed hard, trying to find words to tell him he didn't look in the right place, that she wasn't hard to find.

He smoothed back her hair from her cheek. "Let's go to the house where we can talk. Gunther will take care of your van."

"Wait, Nicholas."

"You were looking for me, weren't you? Otherwise, how would you ever have wound up out here?" His smile was so tender it threatened to bring tears back again.

"Yes, but, Nicholas, why?" Her question was interrupted by a tiny whimper from the front seat of the van.

Nicholas raised his head to glance in that direction,

and his arms tightened, then slowly released her. He looked questioningly at her and pushed her away to take one step to the door of the van, leaning inside.

He reached toward the blanket, turning the edge back to look down into bright blue eyes beneath blond streaked hair. Nicole smiled at him and gurgled, a tiny hand waving at the air around her.

For a stunned moment, he didn't speak. She jumped as he whirled on her. "You didn't let me know?"

She was unable to speak as, plainly furious, he went on. "I have to be its father," he raged at her. "Haven't you noticed it looks like me?"

She almost choked. "The baby is a girl; her name is Nicole. Yes, I'm aware she looks like you, and yes, you're her father."

She was amazed at the quietness of her voice. Of all the ways she could have imagined meeting Nicholas again and introducing him to Nicole, this was never in any of her imaginings.

"Why? Why didn't you let me know?" he demanded. Laughter bubbled up in her throat, laughter coupled with tears that were dangerously close to spilling because she was suddenly exhausted. In the past thirty minutes she had located Nicholas Jordan, finding to her astonishment he was not the hard-working logger she supposed him to be but a lumber magnate, living in splendor on an estate she couldn't imagine the vastness of, an estate complete with guard and locked gates no one entered without special permission.

Now he demanded to know why he wasn't informed he was a father, not bothering to tell her how she was supposed to locate him when he hid his identity very well.

He caught her shoulders again, still fuming in his frustration. As he stared down at her, holding her with his big hands none too gently, he must have realized she was being too quiet.

"Sam." He swallowed visibly and turned her with him back to the van. He led her around to the door nearer to Nicole and opened it. The baby tilted her head back inquiringly as they stood looking at her. Both hands waved, and she kicked the blanket away, soft full lips curving upward at one corner in a toothless grin.

Nicholas caught his breath. "She's beautiful," he said.

"Yes," she agreed.

Seeming to shake himself from the shock he was in, Nicholas closed the door and pulled her with him back to the driver's side.

"Let's go up to the house. I'll drive." He helped her into the van and moved away to speak to the guard he had called Gunther.

Hannibal sat studying the figures around her as she would a stage play. It was a curious gathering, and she wanted Samantha to stay to continue with her scratching behind her ears. Samantha's hands were the best for finding the right spot to rub behind the small points of her ears.

She sighed and let her wrinkled body down gently on the warm pavement, waiting. She didn't have long to wait. Her master turned hurriedly, almost stumbling over her, and clicked his tongue at her in an invitation to get into the back seat of the van. Hannibal eyed the small bundle Samantha was now holding and lay on the seat, her five-o'clock-shadowed muzzle folding itself into a mass of wrinkles on her paws. It would be a good ride to the house.

Samantha watched Nicholas as he drove, realizing that he no longer wore a beard but was clean shaven, his hair no longer shaggy but cut in a smooth, thick style not quite touching his shirt collar. The pale green tie with tiny white designs, pulled loose for comfort, matched perfectly the darker green shirt and pants. He turned to look at her, the bright blue of his eyes pinpointed with darker lights.

He shook his head. "I can't believe this." He looked at Nicole, unsmiling, and turned his attention back to his driving.

She half watched the passing scenery as they wound around curves, coming into sight of the house within a few minutes.

It sat on a slope, a wide, white, two-story building with giant columns supporting a porch that went completely across the front. Chipped marble steps led from the drive, forming a ten-step semicircle to the entrance.

Nicholas glanced once at her and the baby she held before he got out of the van and walked around to her side to help her out. Taking the baby from her, he shifted Nicole to his right arm and took Samantha's hand with the other, leading her up the steps.

She followed without a word across the porch to the heavy double door with some sort of family crest emblazoned in gold in the center.

He touched a hidden button, and she heard chimes

ringing through the house. Almost instantly, the door swung inward to reveal a middle-aged man in white shirt and light blue pants similar to Gunther's uniform.

"Mr. Nick." The lined face split into a grin, and he pushed the door back, standing aside to let them enter. He stared at the woman beside Nicholas and the bundle in his arms.

"Good morning, Trevor," Nicholas said, ushering Samantha into the wide hallway. "This is Miss Bridges."

Blinking in the sudden dimness, Samantha murmured a "good morning" in answer to the man's greeting, her eyes going over the thick-carpeted circular stairway leading upward. She didn't bother to count the steps.

"We'll be in the library."

The man nodded and asked, "Would you like something to eat? Coffee, perhaps?"

Nicholas looked at Samantha who shook her head. "Later, Trevor, thank you."

Trevor disappeared and Nicholas took her arm to lead her into a room off the hall. Hannibal followed Trevor, surmising correctly that food lay in that direction.

Nicholas said it was the library, and it was—strongly resembling the size of the one she had used often at Baylor as she pored over references during exam time. She gave the room a brief glance, walls almost solid bookcases, heavy leather chairs drawn up before a fireplace, big like everything else she had seen.

She stepped closer to Nicholas and reached for Nicole. His arm tightened around the baby.

"I need to change her," she said, her voice completely without expression. She had to do something with her hands as her mind sought for explanations.

He released the baby to her, and she put the bag she carried on the floor and laid Nicole beside it.

"There are plenty of bedrooms," he said.

"She's used to this. It won't hurt her."

As she finished changing the diaper, Nicholas reached again for the baby, his face bent to the tiny one whose blue eyes looked into identical ones above her. She cooed, grinning her toothless grin, and tiny hands reached for the smoothly shaven face.

Nicole loved to touch, and Samantha watched her, a strange sensation in her stomach seeing the two people she loved most examining each other closely. She had argued to herself the pros and cons of revealing the baby to Nicholas, but she knew her decision to look for him had been right. She just hadn't been prepared for other things she had found.

"It's time to feed her, Nicholas," she said, taking a small bottle of juice from the bag.

"I'll do it," he said, not looking at Samantha as he took the bottle and sat in one of the big chairs, his eyes still on the baby. Nicole concentrated on the bottle, and he looked back at Samantha, eyes dark, his expression grim.

"Sit down, Sam."

They faced each other, and hungrily her eyes went over the handsome face revealed underneath the thick wiry beard she remembered. His face was thinner than she thought it should be for a man his size, and there were lines around his mouth. They could have been there before but could also have come as a result of the pain he had suffered with the leg.

"Does your leg bother you now?" she asked.

"Sometimes." He took a deep breath. "Why the hell didn't you let me know? I never thought..."

"I wrote you, Nicholas, but the letter was returned with "addressee unknown" written across it."

"When?"

"Almost as soon as I knew," she said.

He studied her stiff figure, still outsized as always but with a tightness to it, her face softened by the sandy hair touching her chin in a modified pageboy, the wide waves barely showing in its thickness. There was a withdrawn look in her eyes—eyes that he remembered laughing at him, eyes worrying when she knew he was hurting.

"To what address?"

"I waited for you to call me as you said you'd do, and when you didn't call, I used the only address that we had listed in the hospital files." There was no accusation in her voice as she spoke.

He closed his eyes briefly, nodding. "I was due to check back into the hospital the week I left you. I wasn't sure if it would be in Los Angeles or Chicago, and I wanted to wait until I knew." He paused. "The team in Los Angeles recommended I go to Chicago, and I was all in favor of it since you thought they were so good."

Nicole stirred in his arms and he glanced down at her before going on. "When I left you, I took a bad cold and it turned into bronchitis. I was pretty sick for a while. It was three weeks before I knew what was going on, and by then the operation on the leg had been scheduled with the Chicago team." His expression was grim.

"I wrote you a letter but you never answered it."

"I didn't get it," she said.

He shook his head in frustration. "I called the hospital, but they wouldn't give me any information about you," he said.

She nodded. "They're not allowed to give out that information."

"I thought I could wait until I was over the operation and then go back to Yakima." Nicole whimpered and pushed the bottle away.

"She needs burping," Samantha told him, getting up.

Nicholas shifted the baby and lifted her to his shoulder, a big hand patting gently on the small back. She watched in amazement as he expertly burped the baby, returned her to the previous position, and gave her the bottle again.

His expression was grim as he looked up at her once more. "I finally went to the hospital in Yakima and talked to Dr. Reston. He gave me your phone number in San Antonio, and I called your mother."

She looked startled as he continued. "She informed me she hadn't seen you since last fall and gave me your address at Young Memorial. Everywhere I looked was a dead end."

Briefly she explained about her story to Dr. Reston as a reason for her leave of absence, smiling as she added, "My mother would never understand the situation, you might say."

He nodded but his eyes darkened. "Tell me about having the baby. How did you manage financially?"

Finances hadn't burdened her. The pain that filled her was his absence and the fact he had never bothered to see if she was all right.

Samantha took a deep breath and rose to walk away from him to the window, pushing aside heavy cream-colored drapes to look out over the grounds surrounding the house.

Casually, so as not to let him know she loved him more now than ever, she told him briefly about the past year.

She turned back to look at him then as she said, "The check sent me by the lumber company was very generous. I thought I was quite well paid." For the first time a note of bitterness crept into her voice, and he lifted his head to watch her.

"Why did you let me think you worked for a living, Nicholas?" she asked, looking around at the vast expensiveness of the room, wondering how many more such as this remained to be seen.

"I do work for a living, Sam," he said, smiling for the first time since they entered the house. "Believe me, anyone who works for Foster works for a living."

He followed her glance around the room. "This house belongs to Foster and Josephine," he told her.

"Where do you live?" she asked, resigned to the fact that he had married Valerie and lived away from home.

"I have an apartment closer to the business."

There was no need to avoid the next question. "Are you married?"

His eyes widened as he looked at her. He shook his head and placed the baby on the couch beside him before he stood up and walked toward her.

"I'm not married. No, Sam, I guess I was still waiting for you."

Chapter Ten

Standing there looking down at her, Nicholas ran a big hand over neatly combed, thick streaked hair. She missed the shagginess.

"I'm sorry, Sam. I'm sorry as hell." He turned once more to look down at the baby. "Not that it does you any good now."

"We've done all right," she told him, adding, "I was trying to find you before I have to go back to work next month."

He whirled. "You aren't going back to work," he said, his voice dark as the thundercloud in his expression. "The baby has to be looked after."

"She also has to eat," she reminded him.

Nicole slept, unaware of the storm going on around her. "How do you know so much about handling a baby?" she asked as he continued to glare at her. He showed no awkwardness as he burped Nicole and fed her, unusual in an unmarried male, she thought.

"Noelle has two hooligans who require a lot of their uncle's attention." He stood over her. "You aren't going back to work, Sam. I'll take care of you."

She looked back at him, refusing to be intimidated. "And Valerie?"

His mouth tightened, making him look older, or maybe it was because he was clean shaven. "She'll understand."

"I wouldn't if I were she."

A phone rang somewhere in the house, and a moment later Trevor appeared in the open doorway. "Miss Valerie, sir."

Nicholas shrugged impatiently and walked to the wall where a shelf miraculously appeared with a phone. "Hello?" He listened, giving low-voice answers, before he hung up the instrument. Samantha waited, watching him.

"I'd forgotten I had a luncheon appointment with Valerie." He stared at her. "Stay here until I get back. We have to talk."

She wanted to refuse, but she was tired and the baby needed something more solid to eat. "I need to heat some baby food for Nicole," she said by way of agreeing.

"Trevor will do it," he said, reaching for a concealed bell along the wall by the fireplace.

A moment later Trevor appeared and she handed him two small jars.

"I can go into the kitchen to feed her. It's much easier for me that way."

He started to object, but looking at her face, he nodded. "I'll show you," he said.

She looked at Nicholas. He nodded and said, "I'll be back in a short while."

Samantha followed Trevor through a formal dining

room rivaling the Waldorf-Astoria for size and into a sunny, spacious kitchen that was a space-age marvel of appliances and counters. Trevor was placing jars in a steaming bowl.

Nicholas spoke behind her. "Fix Sam some lunch, Trevor. Show her to the front bedroom downstairs when she's finished."

"Yes, sir." Trevor gave her the jars, and she removed the spoon from the carryall bag and sat down in the chair Nicholas pulled out for her.

"You and Nicole can rest until I get back, Sam," Nicholas said. He waited and when she didn't answer him, he turned away.

She didn't look up as he left, conscious of Trevor hovering over her and the baby. "She's beautiful, Miss Samantha." He cleared his throat and backed away.

"I'll get you some lunch," he said.

"I'm not hungry and, Trevor, I've never heard anything so awkward as 'Miss Samantha.' Nicholas calls me Sam and that will do."

A look of horror came over his patrician features. "I couldn't do that. Mr. Nick would murder me."

She grinned at his earthy comment. "I'm almost as big as he is and it's my name. Please," she said.

The smile that touched his thin lips lay there as though it were on unfamiliar ground. He nodded.

"All right, Sam," he said hesitantly.

Her eyes lit into heather-green brightness as she said, "Much better," and concentrated on feeding the baby who smacked in appreciation of stomach-filling warm food. A few minutes later, feathery lashes fell against the smooth cheek and she slept.

"Right this way, Sam," Trevor said, and she was surprised to see a grin on his face as he took the bag from her and led her down the wide hall through an open door to, of course, a mammoth bedroom.

Holding Nicole protectively close to her breast, she looked around at first-class luxury, a far cry from the cabin in the wilderness. Trevor hovered near the door until she turned, surprised that he was still there.

"If you need anything," he said, "the bell is right there." He pointed to a button on the wall.

She nodded as he withdrew and quietly closed the door. Placing the baby on the huge bed, she sat down to kick off her shoes and stretch out beside her.

"Mission accomplished," she said softly to the baby. "Now what happens?"

It was easy to see that Nicholas was shocked at her sudden appearance with the baby, but he showed no signs of doubt that he was Nicole's father. The look of anger in his eyes, whether at her or the circumstances, had never been explained in the short time they talked.

He was still at Valerie's beck and call, and she bit her lip thinking of the reaction he would get if he revealed she was there with his baby.

"I'd be madder than the proverbial hatter," she said, turning to look at the beautiful baby lying there, product of her love for Nicholas in a thoughtless moment.

The tenderness of that love was something she could never be sorry for, but Nicole would be the victim. Nicole should be the one to share in the wealth so obvious here, but because of one unguarded week, she would be denied that.

"I won't let you go hungry, sweetie," she promised,

"but you won't sleep on a bed such as this one nor have Trevor wait on you hand and foot." She sighed. "It won't hurt you, but I may feel that I cheated you out of a lot of worldly goods."

A knock on the door roused her and she sat up, surprised that she had slept along with Nicole. Glancing at the still sleeping baby, she went to open the door to face Valerie.

Shocked surprise made her reactions slower than usual, and she moved aside as the woman pushed past her into the room.

Without a word, she marched to the bed and looked down at Nicole. When she turned to face Samantha, the beautiful face was drawn with anger.

"So," she said, "this was your plan behind a week in the wilderness with Nick." Lips drawn back, she raked Samantha with dark eyes as she searched in her bag, coming up with a slim gold cigarette case. She continued to look at Samantha as she lit the cigarette, tilting her head slightly back to blow smoke upward. She watched the thin blue line disappear into the air, waiting for Valerie to speak again.

She didn't have long to wait. "How did you manage to get him back to the cabin is what I'd like to know?" Her glance said volumes about her ability to attract someone such as Nicholas Jordan.

Samantha took a deep breath. "We met again by accident."

The woman laughed. "I'm sure it was. By your plan, no doubt." When she got no reply to that, she went on, "Why Nick believes you is another thing." She looked back at Nicole, taking in the thickening dark-blond streaked hair and fair skin, any of which could belong to Samantha alone.

Samantha moved away from the door toward the bed. "Did Nicholas discuss the baby and me with you?"

The dark head lifted. "Of course. Nick, the gentleman. Nick, the gullible."

Valerie took a long drag from the cigarette and crushed it out in a small porcelain ashtray on the nightstand. "He's quite upset at having to face someone who's obviously trying to use a tiny baby as a whip to force him to marry her. You're wasting your time." She shook her head. "However, just so we can settle this and get it out of the way, how much do you want?"

Nicole had whimpered and Samantha started around Valerie to check her. At the insulting tone of her voice, she stopped and whirled toward the other woman.

"What?"

Valerie smiled. "Nick is prepared to meet any reasonable demand."

Her throat closed over the outraged retort forming, and she waited a moment before answering. "Nicholas sent you to bargain with me?" she asked finally.

A slim foot tapped soundlessly on the thick carpet. "He had an appointment, but he wanted me to write you a check so you could be gone with the child before he gets home."

"I don't believe you." Nicholas Jordan was not a coward, whether facing nature's fury or the self-proclaimed mother of his child. He would never send someone else to do his dirty work.

Valerie's hand went into her bag again, this time

emerging with a leather-bound checkbook, which she threw on the bed beside Nicole.

Slowly Samantha picked it up, her eyes resting on the gold letters at the corner: Nicholas F. Jordan, Jr. Her breath hurt her chest, and a squeezing pain threatened to cut it off completely.

Placing the checkbook aside, she opened the bag with Nicole's clothing in it and removed a diaper. As she worked over the baby, bright blue eyes looked straight up at her and a smile of recognition curved her soft mouth. She gurgled, tiny hands waving in the endearing characteristic that Samantha loved.

Holding Nicole close to her, she faced Valerie. "You can tell Nicholas for me that I don't need his money. I thought he might like to know about the baby, that's all." It even sounded phony to her own ears, and she smiled a little at the contemptuous expression on Valerie's face.

"I told you that Nick's very generous and he can afford it. Take the money. I'm authorized to sign a check—up to a certain amount, of course."

Without answering, Samantha took the diaper bag, walked around Valerie, and opened the bedroom door. She hadn't thought of asking for money. Beyond finding Nicholas to tell him about Nicole, she hadn't given a thought to anything, but it hurt just the same to have him send a check by Valerie of all people.

At the door she turned. "It must have been painful for you to have to bring the money to me, and I appreciate that. In your place I'd have been fighting mad and slapped his face for the insult." She smiled. "Tell Nicholas the mistake was mine, and I'll take care of it." She went into the hall, leaving the bedroom door open behind her.

Confused for a moment by doors leading in all directions, she found the curving stairway and walked around the end of it to the entrance. It loomed in front of her, and she stood trying to figure out how to open the heavy panels.

"It's getting late to take the baby out, Miss...uh, Sam," Trevor said behind her. "Let me walk her a bit."

She turned to look into the proper features of the butler and smiled. "If you'll open the door for me, please."

"Of course, but..." he started to say.

Behind them, Valerie interrupted. "I'll open it for her, Trevor," she said, but Trevor stepped ahead of her, turning a brass knob Samantha hadn't seen until then, and the door swung inward.

"Mr. Nick called a little while ago to say he'd been delayed and would be here within the hour," Trevor told her, his expression blank as he looked from Samantha to Valerie. He reached for Nicole. "I can heat some food for the little one."

Shaking her head, Samantha moved toward the opening that led outside and to the familiar van parked where Nicholas had left it in the driveway.

She needed to get away from the awesome splendor of the Jordan home and back to the simple things of life, back to caring for Nicole alone, back to her job where complications had a way of working themselves out if one thought them through. There was still enough daylight left to get her past the city, headed toward Yakima, and home before too late.

Concentrating on getting Nicole settled in the front seat, she ignored the two people who followed her down the brilliant white stone steps, but she looked around at the screech of brakes behind her van. Nicholas stepped out, viewing the scene but an instant before he was at her side.

"What do you need from the van? Trevor can get it for you," he said reaching for Nicole.

Her throat hurt from holding back her tears, disappointment alive in her from the insulting way Nicholas handled the money offer. She stood between him and the baby.

"I don't want anything from the van nor from you, Nicholas. Neither of us does." She looked at Valerie's svelte lines in the pink linen dress that cost a fortune. How it must have shamed Nicholas to admit to making love to a woman with Samantha's generously proportioned figure. *Well, now we're even,* she thought. *I'm ashamed of you for your offer.*

"I didn't want to deny you your right to know about Nicole, but your reaction puts my mind at ease. Give your check to someone who needs it. Thank you, anyway." She lifted her head to look straight into his face.

But Nicholas wasn't looking at her. His hands came out, grasping her big arms so that she couldn't move, his touch firm but not rough enough to hurt her. He was looking at Valerie still standing four steps up the marble stone, with Trevor a few feet away from her.

His voice was quiet but his eyes burned his question,

demanding an answer. "What check?" He looked back at Samantha. "I haven't offered you anything yet. And when I do, it won't be a check."

A gasp came from her throat, and she turned with Nicholas to look at Valerie, who smiled. "Miss Bridges needs money to look out for the baby, Nick, and I told her you'd be glad to help. Heaven knows you can afford to be generous with her and—uh—the baby. She isn't the first one who's tried to get money from you with one crazy scheme or another."

She reached into her handbag and withdrew the slim cigarette case. "The baby resembles her, not you, and tests can be rather conclusive." She smiled with comtempt at Samantha. "Surely you can stay around the area long enough to get positive proof of whether Nick could possibly be the father." She paused dramatically, then went on, "Unless you're afraid of the test results."

His fingers dug into Samantha's arms, and she winced, bringing his eyes back to her face, eyes that looked at her from Nicole's tiny face every day. He let her go and with two strides stood in front of Valerie.

"What did you tell her?" he demanded.

The woman shrugged. "The truth. That you're generous and could afford to pay for the baby, even if it isn't yours."

His big hand raised an instant, and Valerie's eyes widened as his fists clenched and he stepped away from her.

"That's pretty low even for you, isn't it, Valerie?" When she only stared at him, he turned and reached

Samantha as she started to climb into the van, wanting only to get away.

Hands that had an instant before been clenched with anger were gentle as he pulled her away from the door and reached into the seat to pick up a sleeping Nicole, cradling her in the curve of one arm, his other around Samantha.

"We'll talk inside," he said, leading her up the steps around Valerie. He stopped long enough to say to her, "I'd hate to have Vic represent Samantha in a slander suit against you, Valerie. He never loses a case."

Pulling Samantha with him, he strode up the steps, his body a straight line of anger. He didn't speak as he led her into the library again, but she stopped inside the door of the big room and pulled away from him. He looked positively incongruous, holding the tiny baby.

She looked up at him, studying the lines in his face that had been etched there by pain. She was aware that he still favored his left leg.

Abruptly she asked, "Do you believe that Nicole is yours?"

His glance went from the baby to her and back again, and he said softly, "I never had any doubt, Sam. You aren't devious enough to name a baby after a man just on the chance that he'd support you."

"But you sent Valerie with your checkbook to pay me off," she insisted.

His mouth dropped open in astonishment. "What?" He sputtered, then suddenly threw back his head and laughed, startling Nicole enough so that she opened her eyes to stare at the man holding her.

Samantha stared, too. "What's so funny about that?" she demanded.

He shook his head. "That Valerie. I should have known she took the news that I was a father too easily. I left her my checkbook to pay for our lunch and she was to drop it off at the office on her way home. I had an appointment with my lawyer."

He crossed the room to her. "Just in case anything should happen before we get things settled, I wanted you and Nicole to be taken care of, and Vic will see to that. He's the company lawyer and there's none better." He grinned. "There'd better not be, the money we pay him."

She was silent, digesting the news that even before they made any kind of decision he had already acted to protect her and Nicole. Goose pimples broke out on her arms and she shivered. No one had ever gone out of his way for her benefit before Nicholas.

He took her arm and led her to the couch, pushing her down and turning away to touch the button she knew would summon Trevor. He came back to stand in front of her just as the butler appeared in the doorway.

He handed the baby to Trevor. "You and Susie take care of Nicole for a while. She's probably hungry." He reached for the bag Samantha had placed on the floor by the couch. "And needs changing, too." He grinned at the tall spare man who held the child up and touched her soft chin with long, thin fingers.

"Yes, sir," he said without looking at anything but Nicole as he went toward the kitchen.

Nicholas turned back to Samantha. "Now, then," he

said, his expression softening as he sat down by her. "Let's go back aways." He didn't touch her as he talked, but his gaze riveted to her face.

"We won't go into the mix-up that caused you to have to deal with our problem all alone. There were so many times I wanted to know what was happening with you, but I could never find out anything. I thought about hiring a private detective, but I kept thinking that maybe you didn't want me to find you. I thought maybe you didn't care about me enough to keep in touch." He shook his head. "When I finally came back to full consciousness, I missed you almost as much as I missed the pain in that leg after the operation."

"You really tried to find me?" she asked, still uncertain about the outcome of her search for Nicole's father. At his firm nod she said, "Oh, Nicholas."

They stared at each other, each with his own thoughts about their dead-end searches, until Nicholas smiled and reached out to touch her hair. "What made you decide to come looking for me up here?"

She told him about the newspaper article. "The address on the hospital letter was Yarmouth Lumber Company, and even though my letter came back, I thought if I could come up and try one more time..." She stopped and leaned her cheek into his palm that rested against her hair. "It seemed worth the effort to let you see Nicole even though..."

"Even though...?" he prompted.

"Well," she said, hesitating before completing her statement on an exhaled breath, "I wouldn't have blamed you if you didn't believe Nicole was yours."

He winced. "You don't hold a very high opinion of

me, do you? Are you so much in with women's rights that you think men shouldn't have any?"

"Oh, no, Nicholas, I didn't even think about it that way. But Valerie's right; I could be after your money."

"Are you?"

She stopped her roving glance over his face to stare in shocked anger. She stiffened away from him.

"No," she said. "If I had been, I'd have taken the check from Valerie."

"What rights are you prepared to give me then, Sam?" he asked.

"What do you mean?"

"Nicole is half mine. I want joint custody."

A tingle of fear sent icy fingers along her spine. "You can't claim joint custody if we've never been married."

She stood still, watching him as his eyes went deliberately over her tall well-endowed figure. His look brought to mind the slender elegance of Valerie's figure.

"No one will blame you for not wanting to marry a woman my size when you can have anyone you choose with a figure like Valerie."

"Do you still measure love by the size of the persons involved, Sam?"

"No, of course not," she denied.

He continued to watch her as she tried not to show how upset she was over his custody statement. "What is your measure of love, then?"

She wet her lips. "I've never thought about measuring it. I've never been in any position where it was necessary."

"It's necessary now," he told her, moving to close

the distance between them. "We didn't have much courtship prior to our love affair," he said, taking her hands. "I remember holding you and kissing you while I was still too feverish to realize what was going on, and that's why I went back to the cabin. I couldn't get the feel and taste of you out of my mind."

He pulled her up against him. "You stayed with me that week, loving me with feelings that I thought equaled mine, and when I tried to find you again, the frustration āt every turn almost drove me mad. It's been over a year, Sam, and I had given up."

He kissed her soft mouth gently. "Even so, Valerie and I had broken our engagement for the third time, and I was sure I'd never find anyone I wanted to marry after loving you."

Her breath came with difficulty, and she didn't dare speak for fear of interrupting his soft flow of words. "We shouldn't wait too long to marry because of Nicole, but I'll court you for a few days if you really want me to."

He kissed the tip of her nose. "Once you told me that if you decided to marry someone, the engagement would be very short. I plan to hold you to that."

She laughed, a trembly sound that shook her big frame. "Oh, Nicholas, what are you saying?"

"I'm saying I love you. How do you feel about me?"

She leaned against him, her arms going around the thick shoulders, dropping to his waist, tightening there. "I love you, Nicholas, but as Nicole's father, I adore you."

He held her tightly for a long time before he pushed her away to look down into her face, flushed with her feelings.

"A three-day courtship suit you?" he asked.

She nodded, unable to speak as he went on. "Foster and Josephine won't be back in the country until next month, and Noelle and her family are due back from the Netherlands about the same time. Too bad they'll miss the wedding, but we'll allow them to give the reception later. Okay?"

She hesitated. "Maybe we could wait for them. Won't they be hurt if you marry without their knowledge?"

He laughed. "Oh, we'll tell them what's happening, and they'll wish they were here. But mostly they'll be so glad to see me finally get married that they'll give us their blessing any time."

He turned her around toward the kitchen and yelled at the top of his lungs, "Trevor!"

The butler ran quickly down the hall. "Mr. Nick, what's wrong?"

"Absolutely nothing, Trevor. Everything's great. Where's my daughter?"

"Your daughter, sir?"

"Nicole is mine, and Sam has agreed to marry me as soon as a ceremony can be arranged."

The man stared in open-mouthed astonishment, recovering himself with concentrated effort. "Congratulations, Mr. Nick, and Miss..." He swallowed. "I'm glad, Sam."

"Sam?" Nicholas frowned at Trevor.

"You named me. Why shouldn't he call me Sam?"

One look at her face and a glance at the proud Trevor, and he said with a grin, "Why not, Sam?"

From somewhere Susie had produced a bassinet for Nicole, and the baby lay sleeping near the open window in the front bedroom that Nicholas had told Samantha she would be using until their wedding. It had taken all evening for them to settle down after deciding they would be married on Saturday morning, three days away. Just time enough for licenses to be bought and arrangements made for a justice of the peace to marry them.

"Josephine will be horrified," Nicholas laughed. "She thinks if you don't have a religious ceremony you aren't married."

"Maybe we'd better wait, Nicholas," she said uneasily, thinking how his parents and sister would react to her. But Nicholas dismissed her apprehensions with a wave of his hand. He smiled at her, holding her slim fingers to his lips.

"Lovely Sam, beautiful hands, sensitive hands that smooth away all my pains."

She felt his touch from her fingertips through her body to her toes. "Nicholas?" She hesitated at the question forming in her mind.

He drew her down beside him on the bed where she had put the dress they decided on for her wedding dress—a pale, barely yellow shadowed print the salesgirl in the exclusive women's shop insisted made her look slimmer.

"Slimmer than what?" she had whispered to Nicholas, as the girl walked away from them, and was forced to place her hand over his mouth to stifle the deep chuckle that formed in his throat. His kiss on her fingers made her catch her breath, and his eyes darkened as his mouth touched hers briefly there in the shop. She didn't dare look around to see how many observers saw the tender caress he didn't try to hide.

She came back to what he was saying. "What unimportant question are you planning to ask now, Sam? Unimportant unless it's: 'Nicholas, how much do you love me?' To which Nicholas answers: 'More than enough for several lifetimes, and it's already past time to start showing you.'"

He pushed her over on the pillow and leaned forward to place his mouth in the well-defined crevice below the V-neck of her blouse. She held him there, her long fingers smoothing his thick hair down over his neck, sliding beneath his loosened shirt collar.

Since the day before when Nicholas made all the decisions about what was to be done and in what way, the hours whirled by until she was dizzy from papers to sign. The plain gold band she wanted had been fitted, and the dress with matching accessories purchased. If she protested about costs, he kissed her mouth closed, and she was forced to give in to him. He made it so easy to surrender.

Now, held tightly in his arms, she breathed in the smell of him, felt the pounding of his heart against her full breasts and smiled as he lifted his head for a moment, then lowered his face to kiss her. The kiss continued until his arms tightened and his tongue pushed between her parted lips, seeking questioningly.

Streams of warmth ran through her as she moaned softly and her mouth opened, seeking to possess all of him as he was possessing her. His hands moved down her body, pushing aside her blouse, unbuttoning it without releasing her from his kiss. Her hands followed his example, finding the wide chest covered with thick blond hair, searching downward. His belt stopped her but only for a moment, and they were moving together, removing their clothing as though it were a regular routine for them.

"Honey?" The whispered question was answered as her eyes opened wide to stare into blue lights above her. She gasped, holding him tightly.

His arm moved away to push the dress from the bed, their clothing dropped hastily on the other side, and the broadness of his body covered her. Dreams of Nicholas left over from her longing for him through the past year came true as he took her with him into the shimmering kingdom filled with love they shared.

He pulled the spread over them and lay stretched against her, his fingers tangled in the silkiness of her hair. His voice came from deep in his chest as he said, "You have a beautiful body, Sam, and it belongs to me. Don't ever put yourself down to anyone, do you hear me? That's about the last order I'll ever give you."

"Yes, Nicholas," she said against his throat. "I hear you." She turned into him, the hardness of his body a perfect foil for the softness of hers.

Contented for the moment, their bodies rested close together, their thoughts registering only the sweetness of the moment.

Nicholas stirred and nibbled her ear. "You smell like a baby."

As if on cue, Nicole began a soft cooing and gurgling, and they turned together to see tiny hands waving in the air. Nicholas smiled at Samantha, kissed her quickly, and got up to walk over to the bassinet to look at his daughter.

Samantha raised up on her elbow to watch the two of them, Nicholas holding out a long finger and Nicole reaching for it, sighing with contentment as she lay back on the pillow.

Chapter Eleven

Nervously Samantha tried to fasten the single strand of pearls around her neck, but her fingers wouldn't stop shaking long enough for her to find the tiny hook. She bit her lip, glancing at Nicole who lay on her stomach on the bed, tiny fingers picking at the white-on-white embroidery of the spread. It would be terrible if she spit up on the rich fabric, all Samantha needed to enhance her status with a new mother-in-law who was bound to be unhappy with the circumstances.

The staccato knock at the door and Nicholas calling interrupted her efforts, and she turned in relief.

"Please fasten these for me," she said.

Without a word he fastened the pearls, a wedding present from him, and kissed the back of her neck, making her shiver.

"I hope I don't make you cold, Sam. That's not my intention."

"Be serious, Nicholas. I'm scared to death."

He pulled her close. "You're a beautiful bride, darling. Nothing to be nervous about."

He turned her with him to walk closer to the bed,

looking at Nicole, happily kicking her heels and cooing. "Doesn't seem to bother Nicole."

And suddenly she wasn't nervous anymore. Nicholas would take care of all the details, explaining to his parents why they couldn't wait a month to be married until his family was back in the States. He wanted Nicole to have his name as soon as possible, and his parents would agree, he assured her. He was big and capable and didn't seem at all worried that they would be upset if the marriage took place before they arrived home.

"They'll love you, Sam," he told her, his eyes alight with tenderness he had shown since she came to the Jordan mansion.

The brief ceremony went off without a hitch because Nicholas Jordan decreed it would, she had no doubt. In the few days she had been in the household, Samantha had been filled in by Susie and Trevor on some of the details of the junior partner at Yarmouth Lumber. He was junior in years and name only.

Foster, as Nicholas so disrespectfully called him, had turned over the reins of the company to his capable son, and Foster spent his time dragging Josephine on buying trips and public relations excursions to all parts of the world.

The butler and the cook, husband and wife, believed the sun literally rose and set on the son and daughter, lavishing their affection on Nicholas now that Noelle had her own family and wasn't around as often as Nicholas.

The reason for Nicholas being in the wilderness

above Goose Prairie when the fire broke out had finally been explained to her.

Nicholas grinned ruefully as he said, "Valerie and I had just broken up for the second time, and I was beginning to have doubts about being able to know my own feelings. The cabin belongs to Yarmouth and our employees use it for camping. I commandeered it for myself that week to get away from the job and myself, too, I guess." He shook his head. "I didn't mean to take my mind off my ability to know what was good for me in such a hard way."

He was like a little boy, if that could be imagined, and he watched her to see how she would take the news that Valerie had been the cause of his being there.

His voice softened as he went on. "Perhaps I did love her at one time, Sam, but never the way I love you. I never knew the meaning of the word until you came along."

Aware that her mind had shifted away from the softly spoken words of the ceremony, she looked up as Nicholas bent to kiss her, whispering, "Now you really belong to me. I have my own personal masseuse, the loveliest hands in the world."

Samantha smiled, accepting the compliment as he meant her to. Her family was complete now, with Nicole's father a permanent member.

They went to the Jordan mansion to a quiet dinner prepared by Susie, but it was far from simple. She had outdone herself, and Samantha groaned as she looked at the food, not seeing the delicious morsels but the calories that she would consume.

"We go on a diet as soon as we get into our own place, Nicholas," she told him. "I can stand only so much of this."

"The house won't be ready for about two months, Sam, but we'll stay at the apartment until it's finished. I want you all to myself."

She quirked an eyebrow at him. "What about Nicole?"

He grinned. "She doesn't take up much room; she can stay."

"But she's demanding," she reminded him.

"And adorable."

Silently she agreed, looking at the man who was Nicole's father. They were strikingly alike and had become instant friends. She couldn't ask for a happier ending to the saga she had begun with such doubts and confusion.

Nicholas stayed away from the office a week after their marriage, doing what business he was needed for by telephone. The days he was at home passed in a lovely haze as they talked nonstop, exploring each other's lives from day one.

"I wrote Leo a letter and told him I found you, and about Nicole. He called me a few days ago." Nicholas tilted her chin to look full into her face as she continued. "He knew I was in love with you; I told him before I told you."

"Is that right?" he asked. "Who is he that he gets such good news before I do?"

"Well," she said, studying the face coming closer to hers, "he seemed interested." She touched his lips. "He called to let me know Benjy is scheduled for a marrow transplant next month. They have high hopes that it will help him.''

Nicholas held her tightly, knowing the emotional strain all of the happenings had put on her. "I'm glad, darling. We'll go see him when he can have visitors."

And while she was telling all, she even told him about her mother and Emily and their concern about her weight and lack of a romantic interest.

He teased her, his voice lazy. "I think you should write Emily and tell her you were kidnapped by a naked giant in the wilderness. She'd probably think it greatly romantic."

"She wouldn't be far wrong," Samantha told him. "Wasn't I?"

"Yes, but I won't accept any ransom for you."

"Everyone has his price," she said.

"I don't need the money," he said, "so I plan to keep you. Besides, you and Nicole come as a package, and no one has enough money to pay for you."

She put her head back to look at him. "Are you really very wealthy?"

He smoothed her hair away from her forehead. "Why do you ask?"

She frowned. "The house your parents live in. This." She spread her fingers toward the understated elegance of the bedroom they shared. He called the place an apartment, but she called it a condominium, a big one at that.

A big hand urged her head beneath his chin and he pressed his lips into her hair. "We have plenty of money to live on comfortably. Foster and Josephine have a little more than we do, of course." His hand slid down her bare back, cupping her hip, pulling her closer to his hard body, effectively distracting her from finances.

A small sigh escaped her as she fitted herself to him. "What was that for?" he asked.

Running her fingers across his hipbone, the edge of her fingernail scraping his skin, Samantha rooted into his throat, her tongue leaving a moist streak down to the hollow over his breastbone. His quiver of pleasure brought her own silvery response of sensuality as he pressed her mouth to his bare flesh.

One hand slid beneath her, the other encircling her, pulling her closer and closer until their bodies became one, moving slowly together until their cries of ecstasy mingled. He kissed her hard, releasing her back to the pillow but keeping her damp body against him.

"In answer to your question, it's because I love you so much," she said dreamily.

His laugh was full of sleep. "You made me forget the question, sweetheart." In a moment his even breathing told her he was asleep, and she relaxed in his arms.

In the few minutes between waking and sleeping, Samantha's mind drifted to thoughts of her in-laws. She dreaded the meeting, yet found herself anxious to meet the people who made up the family to which she now belonged.

Listening carefully to the way Nicholas talked about them, she recognized the deep caring he felt for Foster and Josephine. When he spoke of Noelle, it was with a special inflection in his voice, and she envied the obvious affection the two shared even though Noelle had a family of her own and lived apart. She had missed that affection growing up with Emily; they had never been close as she thought sisters should be.

Turning her face to his bare chest, she bit gently and Nicholas murmured her name, the last sound she heard before sleep claimed her.

A week later, Josephine and Foster came home and the entire clan was gathering at the Circle for dinner.

"This is worse than getting married," Samantha said, smoothing the light blue dress fabric over her ample hips.

Nicholas turned to smile at her. He had finished dressing and was playing with Nicole on the bed. "What a way to refer to our joyous union, Sam," he said.

"I mean...oh, Nicholas, you know what I mean." She went to stand by the bed, looking down at the large and small of her family. "I don't have butterflies in my stomach, I have eagles flopping around in there."

He sat up, reaching for her, and she dropped to the edge of the bed. He gathered her hands in his. They were cold and he drew them up to his mouth to kiss each finger individually.

He shook his head at her. "I appreciate how you must feel, Sam, but Foster and Josephine are nice people, and if I love you, they can't help but follow suit." He touched her flushed face.

The telegram the newlyweds received from Tokyo when Nicholas wired they were married had been standard, but his parents had, at least, congratulated them. All they said was: "About time. Can't wait to meet our daughter-in-law. Love, Josie and Foster."

"Do you really call her Josie?" she asked.

He shook his head. "Foster calls her that. Josie isn't elegant enough for my mother. Just wait until you meet her."

Samantha swallowed, thinking, *An elegant mother-in-law I have to live up to yet. Isn't Emily enough? And Noelle.* Even the name brought visions of slender beauty personified.

Nicole cooed and she turned to look at the baby. At least here was a beauty they could look at; perhaps she would divert attention from a not-slender-at-all daughter-in-law.

Nicholas stood up. "Well, darling, let's take you to slaughter."

"Nicholas!" she exclaimed.

He grinned. "That's what you look like I'm doing to you. Just thought I'd be helpful."

"Thanks a mint," she said, picking up the bag for Nicole as he carried the baby.

The ride to Orleandro Circle was briefer than she remembered at any time in the past few weeks since their marriage, and they were at the big gate before she was ready.

Gunther leaned nearer the car to speak to them. "Well, Nick, your parents look great." He grinned, looking at Samantha and Nicole. "They can't wait to meet your family." He straightened. "And by the way, Noelle took Hannibal up with her."

"Noelle?" Nicholas asked, surprised.

"She and Bruce came in about an hour ago."

"Hey, that's great." He turned to Samantha. "At least you'll have someone nearer your age you can talk to about kids and things." He winked at her. "And dogs."

"I never liked dogs until I met Hannibal," she said, talking over her nervousness, adding, "and that was because I had to have someone to talk to before you woke up."

"Besides, she's special," he said.

"I don't know about special; she's certainly different."

"Same thing," he said, and she knew he was talking to keep her from falling completely apart.

Nicholas parked his car near the back of the house and they went in the side entrance into a suite of rooms the Jordans used for casual entertaining. It was where Nicholas brought her several times when he came out to check on the house. Samantha loved the high cathedral ceilings with skylights, heavy beams across the entire width. A wide stone fireplace covered one end of the room, completing the warm atmosphere.

The room was empty, and she breathed a short sigh of relief. Trevor came soft-footed into the room, his eyes on Nicole. He and Susie competed for the right to hold the baby each time they came, and Samantha handed the baby to him, smiling at his eagerness.

"I can remember a time when I got some attention in this house," Nicholas complained mildly.

"Oh, Mr. Nick," Trevor said. "Mrs. Jordan said they'd be right down." He looked at Samantha. "If you don't mind, I'd like to take the baby with me."

She nodded. Maybe it would be less awkward for Nicholas to present his bride before he introduced his daughter.

Reading her thoughts, Nicholas came across the room holding out his hands just as a low voice spoke from the doorway.

"Hello, Nick."

He turned quickly, moving aside so that Samantha was able to see the young woman in the doorway.

She stared, her mouth dropping open in astonishment. This had to be Noelle. Blond hair, streaked with darker blond, framed a lovely face, the focal point of which were startling blue eyes, identical to Nicholas. That didn't surprise Samantha at all.

Her surprise came from the rest of Noelle. She was a big woman, yet a handsome one, wearing a simply cut shirtwaist dress of yellow dotted swiss. She was a woman at this moment caught in the arms of her brother, who turned around and led her to the center of the room where Samantha stood entranced by the scene.

Nicholas was grinning. "My twin sister, Noelle. My wife, Sam."

Noelle's eyebrows raised a bit as she inquired, "Sam?"

"Samantha if you want to be formal," he said, taking her hand and squeezing her fingers before releasing them.

Noelle smiled down at Samantha, something no woman had ever done, as she usually stood head and shoulders—and width—above them. Samantha took the extended hand and smiled back at Noelle who bent and kissed her cheek as naturally as if they had always known each other.

She straightened and looked Samantha over. "I

couldn't wait to meet the woman who finally captured Nick." She shook her head. "I had all but given up on him, but he always knew what he wanted and went after it."

Samantha glanced at Nicholas who stood grinning at the two young women. *You devious monster,* she thought. *You could have told me you were twins and almost the same size.* But she only smiled at him, looking back at Noelle as she talked to Nicholas.

"Bruce and the little apes will be back shortly. They had to go check how many fish are in the lake so they can start luring them in."

"Nick," a voice boomed from the entrance, and the three of them turned to face the couple entering the room.

The voice matched the size of the man. He was every bit as tall as Nicholas and heavier, his face fuller with age, a shaggy head of silver-blond hair, and blue eyes only a trifle faded with the years.

As father and son hugged and shook hands, grinning at each other with obvious pleasure, Samantha's glance went to the regal lady beside Foster who smiled almost a shy smile at Samantha.

She swallowed, eyes swinging to Nicholas, and back to Josephine. He was right; Josie wasn't nearly elegant enough for his mother. As tall as Noelle, not quite as generously proportioned, Nicholas's mother made Samantha seem small by comparison.

Nicholas turned from Foster, pulling her forward. "My wife," he said simply.

"By God," Foster roared, glancing from Samantha to Nicholas, "you have as much sense as your father."

He reached for Samantha, hugging her in a bone-crushing embrace. Pushing her away, he looked into her eyes that were now wide and incredulous and turned to look over his shoulder at his son.

Laughter shook his big frame. "I take it you didn't warn her about the Jordan giants."

Nicholas grinned in agreement and reached for Samantha, dragging her toward his mother who still stood near the door.

"Josephine," he said, kissing his mother's cheek. "Sam."

"Such a tiny thing, Nick," she said, laughing softly. "We'll all have to look out for her that she doesn't get stepped on." And Josephine hugged her new daughter-in-law as though she had always known she would be her son's choice.

Samantha was trembling as Nicholas took her arm. "The other member of the family is in the kitchen," he said.

"Don't tell me you've bought another one of those ugly dogs like Hannibal," he protested.

Nicholas shook his head. "But I plan to breed Hannibal soon. I found somebody who has a male just like her."

Foster groaned. "How do you propose to feed a litter of vacuum cleaners?" he asked, and Samantha grinned at her own description of Hannibal.

Before either of them could say more, Trevor appeared in the doorway with Nicole, and Nicholas reached to take her.

"Thanks, Trevor. We won't be long." The butler nodded and disappeared down the hallway.

Without a word Foster and Josephine stepped closer to Nicholas, their silver heads bent above the blond head of the baby who stared at them with wide, blue eyes. Josephine extended a tentative finger toward Nicole, and with a juicy smile the baby waved her hand, completely captivating the grandparents.

"Oh, Nicholas, she's beautiful," Josephine breathed. She looked first at Samantha, then at Nicholas, before she said, "Why didn't you tell us?"

"Sam thought one shock at the time was enough," he said, sending a tender glance toward his wife.

Foster frowned. "Did you know about the baby and wait all this time to marry Sam?" His voice was close to disapproval as he eyed Nicholas.

"No, she was a secret from me, too, but Sam's generous and decided I should know about her. I would never have forgiven her otherwise," he said, his eyes still on Sam.

Her breath was tight in her chest as she watched the scene in front of her. Since meeting Nicholas, each happening was different from anything she had ever imagined possible. Meeting his parents and presenting them with a granddaughter at the same time was far beyond her comprehension.

Noelle stepped forward into the pause in conversation and reached for Nicole. "Lord, Nick, she's beautiful. Heaven help me, Bruce will want to try for a girl, now." She turned to Samantha. "We have two boys as wild as their Uncle Nick. A gentle little girl is what we need, I guess," she finished doubtfully. She shot a glance at Nicholas. "You did that on purpose," she accused him.

"Not exactly," he said, his eyes on Samantha, unashamedly loving her.

A clamorous entrance interrupted whatever might have been said as two small boys, perhaps four and five, tumbled into the room followed by a more sedate man.

Noelle sighed. "Basil and Bruce, Jr.," she told Samantha. She moved to meet the man who was her height but slimmer. "Bruce, Sr.," she said, touching his cheek with her lips and smiling as she pulled him toward Samantha. "Nick's bride."

A shy smile showed as he extended his hand to Samantha, giving her a firm handshake. A bashful one in the hardily outgoing group stuck out like a sore thumb.

Further conversation was limited as the two boys clamored for attention. "Mommy, Mommy," the smaller boy, Basil, said, pulling on Noelle's dress. "We found fishes and fishes and frogs and..."

"Tadpoles, Basil," Bruce, Jr., corrected his baby brother with lofty superiority.

"Anyway, can I catch them and bring them home?" Basil insisted.

Noelle shuddered. "No, Basil, not until we get rid of the lizard and the white mice and the gerbils and the hamsters and whatever else lurks under beds and in drawers."

Foster laughed his deep laugh and stepped forward to catch each boy by the hand. "Let's eat. I'm starved."

Nicholas drifted back to link his arm with Samantha's, and Noelle carried Nicole, looking down and talking baby talk to the cooing baby in her arms.

Epilogue

What a mess, Samantha thought, smiling as she looked around the room. She always planned to have a home that looked lived in and, boy, had she succeeded! The clutter surrounding her was the remains of Nicole's second birthday party.

At the moment, Nicholas, Nicole, Basil, and Bruce, Jr., were down at the stables with the pony Foster and Josephine had given Nicole for her birthday. In another stable nearby lay Hannibal with her litter of three Chinese Shar-pei puppies, tiny individual bags of golden wrinkles.

She shook her head in wonder at the past short months. In the house Nicholas had built for them, she had all the love she'd ever wanted from the Jordan family.

And, like Noelle, they were rapidly collecting a menagerie. Samantha was of the opinion that pets were great for some people, but she liked them in kennels.

Mittie, their housekeeper, came through clucking and picking up things and clearing away debris. Noelle and Bruce had left with the promise they would pick up the boys later after their next helping of ice cream.

"They'll all have bellyaches," Noelle said, leaving them behind with relief. She would soon have that little girl Bruce wanted if the gods were kind. Her big body was getting difficult to carry around.

"The mail, Sam," Mittie said, placing several letters on the table she had wiped clean.

"Thanks, Mittie," she said, picking up the envelopes to leaf idly through them.

There was one addressed in Emily's executive secretary handwriting. She opened it first, noticing the postmark didn't look like San Antonio. Holding it closer, she tried to read the cancellation marking.

"Hawaii?" She ripped the envelope open and a picture fell from it onto her lap. She gazed at the couple in the photograph and was still sitting there with the letter in her hand when Nicholas came in alone.

"Are you still eating, sweetheart?" he asked, running his finger under her collar around her hairline. She lowered her head, capturing his hand beneath it.

"No. Mittie took it all away from me," she said. "Where are the children?"

"Bruce came for the boys, and they're all looking at the puppies." He slid both hands down the front of her, caressing her breasts, and she tilted her head back to look at him.

Heavy lids hid the bright blue of his eyes, but she saw the tender curve of his mouth, telling her he was experiencing pleasure from touching her. And she would never be able to paint the picture of the glow he brought her with the light caress of his fingers.

"Happy?" he asked.

She didn't answer right away, but continued to look up at him. His hand came upward over the column of her throat, holding her chin as he bent to place his mouth on hers, ever so lightly, whispering to her.

"You're so lovely, Sam. No wonder Nicole's so sweet. She's just like her mother."

"Is that right?" she asked, thrilling as always to his words. "I didn't know her eyes had changed to cat-green."

He laughed against her warm, moist lips. "Well, maybe a little of her father." He pulled her to her feet, noticing for the first time the letter in her hand. "Important mail?"

An odd light came into her eyes as she glanced at the envelope and back at him. "It's something you'll have to see to really appreciate."

After a swift hard kiss, he released her to allow her to pull the contents from the envelope and hand it to him. He read the letter first.

"Emily's married? Did you know about it?"

"The letter's the first indication I had," she told him. "There's a picture."

He shook it out of the envelope and stared at it, glancing quickly at Samantha, then back at the picture. A grin started at the corner of his mouth and spread until his eyes crinkled at the corners. His lips twisted as he tried to suppress the smile, but when he turned to look at her, he gave up.

He threw back his head and his deep laughter sounded through the room. Then he reached for Samantha, pulling her against his heaving chest, and her own laughter welled up inside her as they clung together, laughing with uncontrollable and delightful mirth.

Finally he pulled her to a chair, and they sat at the table with the picture in front of them. It was a picture of Emily, her slim, tall figure impeccably clad in white shorts, red polka-dot blouse, and white sandals, her hair blowing away from her smiling face. In the background was a tall hotel with a backdrop of Diamond Head, palm trees, and white-capped surf. Beside Emily stood her husband. He was almost as tall as Emily, a prominent paunch around his short waistline hanging over his shorts.

They gazed in silence at the picture until Nicholas asked, "Didn't she tell you who he is?"

"Mr. Gower, her boss at the utility company." She hiccupped and giggled again. "I always pictured Emily marrying a tall, handsome cowboy who might not ride the open range, but at least the mechanical steed at Gilley's."

"Think she'll put him on a diet?" he asked.

"I have no doubt she will," Samantha said, breathing a regretful sigh. "Poor Mr. Gower."

"Poor Mr. Gower," Nicholas repeated. "He had to marry Emily because I married Sam, the beauty of the family."

She gave him her "I love you most of all" grin and leaned across the table to kiss him as the door burst open to admit Bruce and the children.

Moonlight filtered through the sheer curtains at the wide bay window of their bedroom. Samantha lay on her side watching Nicholas sleep, firm lips slightly parted, left that way from their last kiss. The moonlight made patterns across the wide planes of his face, shadowing half of it. She didn't need light to know every millimeter of his face, as well as his body.

Lifting her finger to touch his lips, she gazed into eyes suddenly opened wide. Her finger remained suspended in midair as they stared at each other.

"Go ahead," he said quietly. "I need a massage and you can start there."

Placing her finger at the corner of his mouth, she drew it across to the other side, going upward alongside his nose to the high cheekbone beneath his right eye. From there her fingers skimmed to his temple, remaining as she kissed her way to the curve of his chin. The pulse speeded up beneath her fingers as she licked at the roughness of his late-evening beard.

As he turned on his back, the flat of her palm lay against his cheek, and she slid it downward to his bare chest, through the dark blond tangle of hair over his hard stomach to his thighs.

His breath caught, but he lay still as she raised up to kneel over him. Pressing into his thighs with strong fingers, she used the heel of her hand to circle his kneecap. She dug into the calf of his leg, finding pressure points in the anklebone, sliding both hands around his foot, rubbing with force until he whispered her name.

Without pausing, she went to his other foot, working her way back up the leg with measured movements to his thigh. She raised her head to look at him and saw his teeth flash in a satisfied smile.

He pulled her up on top of him, gathering her body

in both arms until the breath of one was no longer distinguishable from the other. The trembling of his body extended to hers as she half knelt over him, taking him inside her, completing the two halves that made a complete entity of their love.

His big hands came up to catch her shoulders, to push them up so that he could look into her face. "This is love, Sam. This is what people look for all their lives, and it's all mine."

"Share with me, Nicholas," she whispered, lowering her mouth to his. "Love can only be measured when it's shared."

Arms tightening around her brought them together, the sweetness they experienced bringing a cry of joyous fulfillment from two hearts with their full measure of love.

Yours FREE, with a home subscription to

HARLEQUIN SUPERROMANCE T.M.

Now you never have to miss reading the newest HARLEQUIN SUPERROMANCES... because they'll be delivered right to your door.

Start with your **FREE** LOVE BEYOND DESIRE. You'll be enthralled by this powerful love story...from the moment Robin meets the dark, handsome Carlos and finds herself involved in the jealousies, bitterness and secret passions of the Lopez family. Where her own forbidden love threatens to shatter her life.

Your **FREE** LOVE BEYOND DESIRE is only the beginning. A subscription to HARLEQUIN SUPERROMANCE lets you look forward to a long love affair. Month after month, you'll receive four love stories of heroic dimension. Novels that will involve you in spellbinding intrigue, forbidden love and fiery passions.

You'll begin this series of sensuous, exciting contemporary novels...written by some of the top romance novelists of the day...with four every month.

And this big value...each novel, almost 400 pages of compelling reading...is yours for only $2.50 a book. Hours of entertainment every month for so little. Far less than a first-run movie or pay-TV. Newly published novels, with beautifully illustrated covers, filled with page after page of delicious escape into a world of romantic love...delivered right to your home.

Enter a uniquely exciting new world with

Harlequin American Romance ™·

Harlequin American Romances are the first romances to explore today's love relationships. These compelling novels reach into the hearts and minds of women across America... probing the most intimate moments of romance, love and desire.

You'll follow romantic heroines and irresistible men as they boldly face confusing choices. Career first, love later? Love without marriage? Long-distance relationships? All the experiences that make love real are captured in the tender, loving pages of **Harlequin American Romances.**

What makes American women so different when it comes to love? Find out with **Harlequin American Romance!**

Send for your introductory FREE book now!

Get this book FREE!

Mail to:

Harlequin Reader Service

In the U.S.
2504 West Southern Ave.
Tempe, AZ 85282

In Canada
P.O. Box 2800, Postal Station A
5170 Yonge St., Willowdale, Ont. M2N 6J3

YES! I want to be one of the first to discover

Harlequin American Romance. Send me FREE and without obligation *Twice in a Lifetime.* If you do not hear from me after I have examined my FREE book, please send me the 4 new **Harlequin American Romances** each month as soon as they come off the presses. I understand that I will be billed only $2.25 for each book (total $9.00). There are no shipping or handling charges. There is no minimum number of books that I have to purchase. In fact, I may cancel this arrangement at any time. *Twice in a Lifetime* is mine to keep as a FREE gift, even if I do not buy any additional books.   154-BPA-NAWB

Name _____ (please print)

Address _____ Apt. no. _____

City _____ State/Prov. _____ Zip/Postal Code _____

Signature (If under 18, parent or guardian must sign.)

AMR-SUB-2